PRAISE FOR *BULFINCH*

"I was astonished at the depth of emotion conveyed in the book. I felt the same way after reading *Queens of All the Earth*. Sternberg has such a talent for examining and sharing these deep, deep emotions in such a way that readers get swept up in them as well. The word that came to mind when I read this book was delicious. I felt like I was devouring it and that it was just delicious."
-Allie Duzett
-Author of *The Body Electric*

"I'm a sucker for books about knights and monks, and in this delightful tale, a suitably belligerent knight and dreamy monk help a very modern girl solve her very mysterious problems in a very medieval way. Highly recommended."
-H.W. Crocker III
Author of *The Old Limey*

"Meticulously researched, through nifty writing and the art of fantasy, Sternberg brings a couple of characters from the Middle Ages to the present and to life. A terrific read."
-Gary Alexander
Author of the Buster Hightower mystery series

Bulfinch

a novel by
Hannah Sternberg

ISTORIA

IB

BOOKS

DEDICATION

for Dad

if every friend became his foe
he'd laugh and build a world with snow.

- E. E. Cummings,
"my father moved through dooms of love"

CHAPTER ONE

Lord Henry shrugged his shoulders. "My dear fellow, medieval art is charming, but medieval emotions are out of date. One can use them in fiction, of course. But then the only things that one can use in fiction are the things that one has ceased to use in fact...."

—Oscar Wilde, *The Picture of Dorian Gray*

UNCLE ALVIN ANSWERED the phone. I was still afraid of it. Uncle Alvin was also afraid of the phone, but he'd had several decades' more experience answering it despite that. So he was the first to hear the news.

It was four in the morning in Baltimore, which meant it was ten in the morning where my parents were supposed to be. Except they weren't there.

Nowhere to be found ... highly unusual ... searched the entire ship ... cannot delay embarkation any longer....

I heard these snatches in the high, tinny voice on the phone's earpiece. Uncle Alvin always had it turned up very loud. He didn't say much in return.

I sat on the third step from the bottom of the stairs, listening to Uncle Alvin on the phone in the kitchen. The only light on was the little orange one on the phone desk.

"How long?" I heard Uncle Alvin grunt.

I strained, but I couldn't hear the tinny voice's response.

"And where would that be?" Pause. "Hrmph. And if they just overslept?"

Assure you ... itinerary ... next port ....

"When was the last time they were seen?"

"..." I heard the tinny voice but couldn't make out its words.

"Thursday," Uncle Alvin said.

My heart pounded so hard it hurt. Thursday was the last time my mom had called, from a hotel phone in a resort on the Mediterranean. My parents were on a European tour and cruise. It had been a surprise anniversary gift from my dad. I'd been deposited with my Uncle Alvin two weeks ago, to be held until they returned.

My pulse drummed so loudly in my ears I missed the rest of the conversation. I heard Uncle Alvin put the phone back on its cradle. He sat in silence for a while. Then, even though I was around the corner and out of sight, he said, "Come in here."

I stood, surprised by how stiff my knees were. I'd been sitting, without moving a muscle, for longer than I'd realized. I wobbled into the kitchen. Uncle Alvin didn't say anything but looked at me while I stood, arm's length away, for a long minute. His face said nothing.

Then Uncle Alvin stepped forward and hugged me. He had never hugged me before that I could remember.

I was twelve. That was seven years ago.

It would be seven years before I learned that time travel really is possible, but in those years I traveled to that moment many times in my mind, always trying to change it and failing.

❧❧

The summer I was twelve, before my parents dropped me off at Uncle Alvin's, life was more than perfect. Life was so good it hurt. Nothing bad had ever happened ever, and I always ran to pick up the mail when I heard the mailman honk.

Our box was always full of junk. Every once in a while there'd be a bill or a package from Uncle Alvin. Uncle Alvin's packages usually consisted of pens advertising prescription medicines, plastic letter openers with magnets on the back, and stale oyster crackers. I stopped getting excited about Uncle Alvin's packages by age eight. But I loved flipping through every single page of any catalogue that arrived at our house.

On a shiny Wednesday afternoon, The Letter fluttered out of the mess of glossy coupon fliers as I lifted them out of the mailbox. I saw it catch the sunshine like a sail as it went down, and I picked it up from the dirt. It was crinkled, with a small rip near one corner, and it was paid for with a collection of two-cent stamps—there were twenty-five, and they filled nearly a third of the front of the envelope. The ink-stamp of the sending post office was smudged and unreadable. There was a tea-colored, ring-shaped stain on the back of the envelope, to the right of the center. On the front, the receiver's address was handwritten in blue ballpoint:

Joe Creekman
16 Beauview Drive
Whitehall, MD 21161 USA

There was no return address, though in the upper left corner was written "Vita."

I brought it to the dim living room (the shades were pulled down to keep out the heat) and showed it to my mom.

"Well, that's interesting," she said. "I didn't know there was a Beauview Drive." We lived at 16 Beauview Road.

"Let's get out the map," Mom said. She bounded to the garage and came back with the big Harford County map that lived in the backseat of her car. I scanned through the index like she'd taught me and found Beauview Drive.

"Now it's time for an adventure," my mom said.

We lived in a rural area, with eight acres all to ourselves, a huge vegetable garden, and a rabbit warren. The farms of our county were wide and lush, surrounding surprising pockets of gentle, civilized forest in depressions or on the hills swelling here and there. In my memory, it was the land of safety and goodness, the only land there was.

Sometimes those days, I was frustrated with our little woods, nothing like the deep mysterious forests of my fantasy novels. I used to imagine that being plunged into the supernatural would excite me. I never thought that after the strange found me, I would miss this comfort and predictability.

But I am sure that, on that day, as we ventured from Beauview Road to storm the strongholds of Beauview Drive, I was happy. We drove for twenty minutes, taking lazy back roads, winding through quilt-square fields with the windows rolled down. A fantasy novel was sitting wrinkled on my knee; I never went anywhere without my book. We had the oldies radio station turned up, and my mom's perfume filled the car. I was thinking of nothing but the present, which isn't thinking, but feeling, and I felt great.

I was a little sad when we turned onto Beauview Drive. And nervous. It was overwhelmingly quiet there, and from the sense of oppression we turned the radio off. The road was narrow and shady, surfaced with smooth packed dirt; it took a turn down near a stream, and the woods around it were preserved, with the houses hiding shyly on the edges. They were woods of space and light, tall narrow birches with airy translucent leaves. The ground beneath them was a sea of lacy ferns. It looked like a cathedral.

Beauview Drive was not a long road, though the houses were spaced comfortably far apart. My mom and I counted them as we passed each one, reading its number from the mailbox or the front door. It was a chant meant to heighten excitement as we approached the secretive abode of Mr. Joe Creekman, which is why I felt a supernatural thrill when we coasted to a dead end after only reaching fifteen. We idled at the weed-invaded cul-de-sac, and my mom exhaled a quiet "Huh."

We drove back up the road and then down again without speaking this time, only straining our eyes for the sixteenth house, but there was none. In my mother's bag was a letter addressed to nowhere. We didn't see any names on the mailboxes, and we felt a strange shyness about getting out to look around or ask.

As we drove away from the cul-de-sac one last time, without the intention of coming back, I thought I saw something flash in the woods, like light on polished metal. My fingers curled around my book.

My mom turned the radio back on. Elvis Presley was singing "Return to Sender." We both laughed until our eyes ran.

Later, while we were sitting at a picnic table outside Dairy Queen, it was possible to believe that the summer would last forever.

◦❧◦

Back home, while we lay on an old wool army blanket in the backyard, I wondered about the light I had seen in the woods on Beauview Drive.

It could have been a metal sign. Or a bike's reflector on some secret trail. Or the first scout in the army of knights that was soon to invade my imagination. As if the occupation had already begun, I could see them in those woods, their frayed white tunics blending with the trees, their helmets darkened with the patina of unreality. I would see that light again, years later, and it would change everything.

There was no J. Creekman, no 16 Beauview Drive. The letter was ours.

That's what I told myself when I stole the letter from my mom's tote bag that night, shoving it up the front of my nightshirt and running to my room. I took it out and ran my fingers along the edges, which were softened with wear.

I was afraid to open it, in case changing it in any way would cost me a valuable clue. This must be how modern archaeologists felt about unwrapping a mummy.

But I couldn't wait forever. I opened the letter after I heard the creak and whisper of my parents going to bed. I used a plastic letter opener from one of Uncle Alvin's packages.

Inside was a page torn from a book. The paper was medium-weight, gritty, yellowed more on one edge (the free edge of the page), and lightly notched on the other (the part that must have been stitched into the binding). My breathing was shallow and my heart shot percussive bolts of adrenaline into my dizzy head.

The page was about the size of one of my mass-market sci-fi paperbacks, but the binding edge had a curl to it, as if it had been sewn into a fat volume. I noted this, more smug than Sherlock Holmes. I ran my eyes over both sides twice before I could slow down and focus enough to make the type resolve into words.

This is what I read:

118

off he cried he should never touch the tunic again. His penance was a fast of ten days, which he performed with worthy humbleness, and that very year it pleased God that his wife should become great with child and bear him a son named Robert, whom he pledged to the Church in gratitude for his salvation. Of these things I am assured of their veracity, having heard them from a neighbor and faithful patron of our order, who knew him for many years as a brother and had the story from his own mouth.

52. A KNIGHT ERRANT ERRS.
(Cotton MS 4612, *tome* IV, xxxix–xvi)

At that time, a youth of one of the northern duchies traveled to our shrine, having joined his father in the profession of knighthood. His father was a brutal warrior, the worst of his type, who was known to sever the hands of his enemies after he had slain them and collected his unholy trophies in a row in his hall in a pagan manner.

The son likewise was as many men of our time, Christian in name only, and his purpose in visiting the holy and revered relics of our blessed saint was in the nature of a superstitious bargain, rather than the inspiration of true piety, much as the girls of the village in spring would enact their rites as ever their barbarian forebears had, profaning the sign of the cross by incorporating it into their unruly rituals. This son of a knight was loud at table and vulgar of

speech,

119

speech and spent a day partaking of our hospitality, while he idly hoped to gain good fortune through his mumbled prayers. And it was true that his prayers were not sincere, because he was not inspired to open his purse and make a suitable donation to our shrine, but instead only poured a fraction of the coin into the box, of what was indicated of his wealth by the flagrant sumptuousness of his finery.

And so our blessed saint found it fit to perform a miracle to chastise the pride and selfish parsimony of the young knight. For he made his bed under the low canopy of his cape slung over rough branches that night, in a stupor of dissipation. And in his dreams he was visited by many beautiful maidens in a train, who lifted his canopy and poured a most delightful and terrible light upon his face, and before him stood the image of our blessed saint, in a shining robe of porphyry, and a circlet of diamonds and a cape of gold and silver and all other fine things interwoven, and with a terrible grimace spoke to the young knight of his iniquity and wantonness, and he was filled with fear and awe.

And the next morning, the young knight awoke to find that the fine gems sewn into his tunic were turned to patches, and the gold upon his saddle was grime, and his silks were coarse wool and his purse full of ashes. He rose in a rage, suspecting some cruel prank, but soon discovered he had been transported to some strange and new place, and he was filled again with awe, for he knew that this must be a true miracle of our blessed saint, and his heart was full of sorrow for his misdeeds. So began the journey of the young knight, as I have been told by one who knew him well in his later years, and who had his story direct from its hero. On that day, the young knight resolved to lead a righteous life, as he sought his long way back to familiar lands in order to atone to the poor monks he had abused. But this was only the beginning of his trials, trials to break in his young violent spirit and make it just. For it is said that later on his journey, the youth was seized by a very madness

of

That was where it ended.

Out of my secret page-letter rushed monsters of my imagination. Was I just as bad as the cursed knight, because I had stolen the letter? When I closed my eyes, would I open them again in a new and unfamiliar place? Maybe I could dodge the curse by slipping the letter back into mom's bag while the rest of the house slept.

When I crept downstairs to put the letter back, I knocked over a plant. My dad came down and found me immediately.

I was lectured on the grave importance of respecting other people's privacy, that it was a felony to tamper with the mail and I shouldn't let it become a habit; that we all lived to learn how to become considerate and polite adults. That bumping around in the middle of the night was very bad and that some of us had to go to work in the morning so we wouldn't be poor and eat only cabbage.

I cried until dawn. The next morning was bleak.

Mom and I sat around inside, the fans whirring and the lamps off, watching soaps. I finished one novel and started another. The weather retained the pathological perkiness of an infomercial host.

By the afternoon, I made a weak joke about fetching the mail. By the evening, Mom seemed to find it was appropriate to satisfy her own curiosity. Dad had a meeting that night, and as I helped carry the remains of our Chinese carryout dinner to the sink, Mom said,

"Was there anything important in that letter? If there was, we should keep trying to deliver it."

"I don't know," I told her. "It was just a page from a book."

Mom's eyebrows shot up.

"Well, since you've opened it anyway, let's take a look."

I didn't have to be asked twice. I dropped my plate on the counter and bolted upstairs to get it. When I came back down, Mom had swiped the table clean of crumbs and puddles of duck sauce, and we sat together with the letter between us on the gleaming surface. Mom picked it up and held it close to her face, reading it twice, before she put it down again and made another one of her contemplative noises, "Huh." When I heard that noise, I knew something really interesting would follow; otherwise, she would change the subject entirely.

"Do you know what it's from?" I asked, because at that age it was still a fact that, between them, my parents had read absolutely everything.

"It's fake," she said. "Or it's from a very, very unique book. The kind that people collect just for its printing errors. I bet that's why this 'Vita' wanted to send it to our 'Joe Creekman,' though she would have destroyed the overall value of the book and the find by taking it apart. Not to mention folding it."

I peered silently at the letter and my mother, waiting for the more that would surely come, and it did.

"See, look. If this edge is where it was bound in the book, then '118' would appear on the right side of the open book and you would turn the page to read '119' on the left side. But nearly every Western book is traditionally printed with the even numbers on the left side and the odd on the right."

"So it's like a page between pages?" I asked, trying to wrap my mind around it.

"It's a misprint. But a very interesting one because the text of the two pages follows logically. It's possible the printer just skipped a page number, or repeated one, or even accidentally reversed the odd-even order of the whole book."

"So Vita tore out the page to show Joe Creekman a funny mistake?"

"It's possible. But it's not the only weird thing about this page. Look at these. Do you know what they are?"

She pointed at the last words of each side, "speech" and "of." I shrugged and shook my head.

"They're called catchwords," she explained. "They're the first word of the next page, printed at the bottom of the previous page with a right-margin alignment. They were used to help the bookbinder, so he knew he was putting the pages in the right order."

I looked at the catchwords with wonder. What a useful little clue! I wished all my books had catchwords. It was like turning the page before you actually had; like the text was pulling the book along, inexorably.

My mom wasn't done, though.

"But catchwords fell out of common use in the eighteenth century. And the typesetting of this page looks like it came from the late nineteenth century at least. I'm not expert, but just look at the letter 's.' It's a classic giveaway. In the eighteenth century and earlier, the 's's in the middle of words, paired with a second 's' or sometimes at the beginning of selected words, were printed with a special elongated character, the one that looks like an 'f.' You've seen those in class, right?"

I had. I had seen at least a dozen replica broadsheets of Revolutionary War documents printed with the funny "s"s, and every year the kid who was asked to read one aloud would say something like "refpect" and the whole class would laugh.

"Well, this typeset doesn't have the funny 's.' Or any of the other eccentricities you find in an eighteenth-century book, except the catchword," my mom continued. "The spellings are even, the type is small and clear. I wonder...."

She looked at it. "I wonder...." was like "Huh." It was her brain sighing. The wheeze of bellows inflating, the first purr of an engine starting.

"This is weird," she said as if the effort of explanation was suddenly too much and got up to fill a glass of water from the kitchen sink. While she did, she looked out the window above the sink, into the dark.

"What do you think the book's about?" I asked tentatively.

"How am I supposed to know?" she snapped. "Tell me yourself." But then she seemed to soften and came back to the table.

"I don't know what book it's from," she said. "But if you want to figure out what it's probably about, just use your brain. Look at it. It has a story about a knight and a monastery somewhere. And paganism is still a living issue for them, evidently. So I'd say it was about early or high-medieval society."

I knew that the Middle Ages came somewhere between Rome and anything I would recognize. I was vaguely aware they were somehow related to Robin Hood. I wasn't sure where King Arthur fit in.

"Now, the first page has the ending of another story. So I'd say it was an anthology or collection of some kind. And this story is numbered, which confirms that. Look at the fine print there under the title, 'A KNIGHT ERRANT ERRS.' It looks like a citation, doesn't it?"

I nodded. My mom had taught me how to read citations by the age of five. I liked them; they were neat formulae that seemed to place information as surely in the physical world as it could be found on the internet. This is where you have to look, they said, and whenever I followed one to its source, I felt a mild surge of pride and wonder because there it was.

But this citation looked different. I waited for the explanation, which poured from my mother in natural response to my attentive silence.

"This citation refers to manuscript, in a collection called 'Cotton' in the book's shorthand. It probably belonged to a collector named Cotton once or was bought or conserved using an endowment made by someone named Cotton. There are all sorts of ways to read that. But the manuscripts within that collection would be numbered, and this citation tells us which manuscript the passage comes from, which volume, and which page. There's probably a key somewhere at the beginning or end of the book this page came from that gives the full names for all the shorthand citations."

"So it's a story from a manuscript?"

"A medieval manuscript, I should imagine. Otherwise, wouldn't it have its own name, and author, and publisher, and date, so it could be cited the way you're used to seeing?"

I wasn't entirely sure, to be honest, why that was obvious. I wasn't even clear on when printing had been invented, exactly. I knew it was after the Middle Ages (or maybe it was their end?). Did they use funny "s"s back then, too?

"So my guess is it's a sourcebook," my mom continued. "Like the kind students use when they're learning. See, the originals of these things are sometimes hard to find and borrow; and once you do get it in your hands, you might not be able to read it because it's in Latin or a medieval language or a funny script that it takes an expert to decipher well. So scholars compile these sourcebooks that include translations of documents, manuscripts, and stories for students to use in their research and for people to learn from. So you can see the history for yourself rather than getting it through another person's retelling."

"Oh," I said. My eyes ran over the side that was facing upwards, page 119, over and over, like hands knitting or stroking a cat. "So ... it's a true story?"

My pulse pounded, imagining the knight hurtling through space and time toward me.

My mom smiled a little. "I don't know if it's true in the sense that poor Sir Unknown got teleported sometime long ago to a galaxy far, far away," she said, getting up and ruffling my hair, "but it's true in the sense that a genuine medieval monk probably wrote it down in a genuine medieval manuscript somewhere.

"That is," she said, pausing as she refilled her water glass at the sink, "Unless the whole page is a fake."

She shuffled toward the living room. I heard the TV turn on. I sat in the kitchen holding my knight. On his page.

It was sudden like a flood, certain as the stars hide behind clouds. At that moment, the Middle Ages marched into my imagination, set up camp, and proceeded to pretend they'd always been there. It was so natural I barely noticed. Vivid little monks, knights, and barbarians meandered through my mental landscape, blending in with the scenery.

I was allowed to wait up with Mom for Dad to come home that night, which seemed like a treat I didn't deserve considering I'd committed a felony the previous night. But that was forgotten now; how I found the letter meant little, it was already the distant past; what I had gained from it was more important.

As I climbed into bed at 10:30, lowered down from my mother's arms at the threshold to my room, I knew that I would dedicate my life to the study of the Middle Ages. I didn't have to think about it. I knew it as certainly as I knew Mom and Dad would be downstairs eating breakfast tomorrow morning.

Sometimes I wonder what my friend Bulfinch's life was like when he was twelve. Bullied by his punkish knight brother, sheltered by his feeble mother, sneaking books into his garret room under an ill-fitting cloak. Like me, he felt he was friends with the people he read about. Did he also have one sweet unbroken moment of childhood? One summer in the fields of his father's manor or in the shadows of a cool chapel, when he believed his parents knew everything and anything was possible and the world hadn't yet tried to teach him otherwise.

CHAPTER TWO

#34: Child's suitcase
Dimensions: 24" x 42" x 8"
Description: Harlequin-patterned blue and purple
cloth suitcase, two wheels, retractable handle
(broken), zipper padlock (keys lost)

MOM AND DAD were celebrating their twentieth anniversary when they disappeared. Dad had surprised Mom with the trip a week before they left, in one of his extravagant gestures that made Mom blush on birthdays and holidays. He presented the tickets to her with a pair of diamond earrings to wear at the captain's table. I ogled the two of them, beaming their megawatt smiles at each other across the table, the two happiest parents a girl could ever dream of.

I wish there was an event that I could describe that would make their disappearance real to you. The first weeks lashed at my eyes and my heart like a stinging rain, chilling, violent; there was confusion, regret, terror. But a disappearance is ultimately a non-event, cumulative, creeping, to those who only wait and wait, and it is the formless uncertainty that only increases the pain. My parents simply ceased to appear one day; and instead of appearance, we had Dis, the darkness of the presumptive underworld, death by invisibility.

I've imagined enough possibilities: an identity mix-up that forced them on the lam for crimes they didn't commit; a freak lightning storm that separated the cliff they stood upon, in a terrified embrace, from the chalky bluff; a ride with a psychotic local fisherman, zealous to add more tourists to his "collection." Or they were lost in a book, the book my mom told me she was about to read in her last postcard to me.

According to the official record, they were last seen boarding a small boat alone on the evening of August 15, near the Zakynthos sea caves in Greece. And I never moved out of the spare bedroom in Uncle Alvin's tiny old row house in Hampden, where pink flamingos nod in front of peeling porches. I never put any posters on the walls. I never scribbled on the top of the desk to make it mine. I never even finished putting my clothes into drawers. Whenever I did laundry, I folded my clothes neatly and stacked them back in my luggage. I knew then and there that if I stopped "staying over" and started living there, my parents would never be coming back. I was keeping them alive. As long as I was waiting for them, I'd never have to mourn.

Uncle Alvin couldn't replace my parents. He was more like a curmudgeonly grandparent—a reclusive widower and semi-retired teacher, he was fourteen years older than my mother. He was short, with a white shock of hair and mismatched argyle socks. He wore all black to simplify wardrobe coordination (I suspected he was secretly colorblind), but random accents slipped in, like a mustard-yellow vest or a neon-green striped tie for special occasions. He wore that tie to my first graduation, and after two hours in a brutal Baltimore heat wave, I thought it had actually begun to wilt.

Uncle Alvin was fiercely dedicated to educating me, as if he were the commander of a military imperative against ignorance and I were the central front. His years as a student and teacher had trained him to distrust institutional learning. He was never interested in my grades, and if I shared them he became positively annoyed. He succeeded in slipping me through high school in two years—with a diploma in my hand, but one that seemed to say, "Please get her out of here, she's making us uncomfortable." I enrolled as an undergraduate at Loyola-Baltimore at the age of fifteen. My social experience was not spectacular.

Once he had accomplished this jab in the eye of the educational establishment, Alvin conscripted me to a project he had been working on silently for decades, a project called "The Catalogue."

Uncle Alvin's house was like a seventeenth-century scholar's *wunderkammer*, if resin snow globes had been invented in the seventeenth century. In it was stored all the debris of his life. Bumper stickers, wind chimes, and dream catchers from the cross-country road trip his family had taken when he was seventeen and my mom was three. Six-page pamphlets on local history with poorly reproduced photographs of villages across Britain, relics of Alvin's year of study abroad in college. Figurines from Mexico and painted mugs from Italy and France that his students throughout the years had brought back for him. Coasters from diners and pens from school fairs. His late wife's knitting was still piled into a basket by the armchair next to the window, sweater half-finished.

The house existed to hold this trove; we simply found enough room to occupy it, so we could do the work of preserving and ordering it all.

It was impossible not to get involved. That first year, when I was twelve, I only noticed that Uncle Alvin liked to spend his evenings quietly sorting boxes from the basement, making notes in a binder with a big Roman numeral on the spine that matched a set arranged on the living room shelf like volumes in an encyclopedia. I watched with incomprehension as he meticulously arrayed his treasures on the shelves of the rooms on the third floor, the Museum. By age thirteen I was a busy worker bee, helping him lift artifacts up and down stairs or building compartmented cabinets out in the garage and mounting them on the Museum walls. Uncle Alvin would hold my arm up in the flex position and call me "Rosie," for Rosie the Riveter, and on my fourteenth birthday, he gave me a spotted kerchief to wear on my head.

After my last day of high school, when most kids were swelling with pride at the thought of becoming sophomores and I was already acquiring my college textbooks, Uncle Alvin bought a box of Berger cookies to celebrate. As I scraped the inch-thick fudge frosting off the top of my third and felt the sugar begin to corrode my insides, Uncle Alvin started to tell me about The Catalogue in detail. I had been a serf before, supplying the Museum's outer needs, but now he let me in on its innermost secrets. He left me for a moment in the kitchen and came back from the living room with the red binder marked with a big black "I."

"This," he said, "is The Catalogue. The numbers aren't meaningful. Each object is numbered in the order that I find it."

He took a sheet of small round stickers from a sleeve inside the binder.

"I put the number of each object on one of these stickers and place it somewhere unobtrusive on the object, so I can match the item to the description in the book. Always mark your number accurately."

He put the sheet of stickers back and turned to the first page of The Catalogue.

"Each item has a name," he continued. "Nothing cute. Then the dimensions. Then a short description."

I looked at the first entry.

1. Wedding Ring
Dimensions: 0.5" diameter, 0.166" thickness
Description: Patti's wedding ring. 14k gold. Smooth surface, rounded edge. Inscription inside: "Darling, you send me." Purchased at Smyth's Jewelers, Baltimore, 1977.

I glanced at the gold ring on Uncle Alvin's left hand. He cleared his throat and flipped over the pages of the first volume of The Catalogue with impressive gravity.

"I could use your help," he said. "You're a smart girl now. Well, nearly. And you'll learn more here than you will in your classes, if your teachers are anything like the ones they had at my college."

This was the only preparation he gave me for my upcoming matriculation. I became incorporated into The Catalogue; as a cataloger or an item, I was never quite sure.

For the rest of my fifteenth summer, I rummaged. I was a natural rummager, but that summer I perfected it into an art. Like Uncle Alvin had said, the numbers were meaningless, so I was free to paw through the mountains of junk in hidden corners and choose the items that most caught my fancy; often they were enhanced by a story told by my uncle, and so in the long run I don't think I saved him much time at all, counting all the interruptions I made with my questions. Words, like progress, are irrelevant anyway because we never plowed forward so much as we plowed through; Uncle Alvin's house, a row home with a footprint a quarter of the size of the home I had shared with my parents and two stories taller, seemed to generate an unending store of secrets and hidden treasures. Eventually I realized we weren't working toward a foreseeable end. Even if we managed to catalogue everything that had been in the house before the project began, it would have taken so long that in the meantime enough new acquisitions would have collected to start a whole new Catalogue.

Outside, teen mothers in torn jeans talked trash over their strollers, and the shoe-mender around the corner dusted his front step and sucked in the first cigarette of the day. Inside, Uncle Alvin and I did the sacred duty of monks, consecrating ourselves to the sacrament of history. In his kooky house, it wasn't difficult to slip into the past, the comforting kind that traveled far beyond the recent tragedy that still throbbed deep.

That summer before I went to college, three years after Mom and Dad were captured by pirates or ransomed by Bedouins (I was still deciding), we rented out my parents' old house in Harford County. Uncle Alvin put the revenue in a savings account for me. We packed up my childhood and moved it to the attic of the little house in Hampden, where the boxes blocked the two tiny windows looking vertiginously down, on the street on one side, our postage stamp of a garden on the other.

I did the only thing that seemed natural in my surreal new life. I catalogued my old one. I did it late at night, after Uncle Alvin had gone to bed, by the light of one incandescent bulb hanging from the ceiling, shaded by a cloud of moths, in the oppressive blanket of heat. As sweat beaded under my thin T-shirt and a delirium of lazy exhaustion weighted my eyelids, I began to believe that what I was conducting was a prayer.

The ancient Egyptians believed that one's soul persisted in the Underworld as long as that individual's name was repeated in the world above. Mom and Dad. Mother and Father. Mama and Papa. Children don't call their parents by their names.

Come home, come home, I sang in my mind. *Come home*, as I wrote each entry neatly and concisely. But it would be several years before I stumbled upon the formula that would translate my longing into reality, and then, I overshot by a few hundred years.

I kept my personal Catalogue a secret from Uncle Alvin. I didn't have to; after all, the house was obviously a catalogue-friendly environment. But I thought he might find it offensive that I have given my Catalogue the capital "C" reserved for his own. I also wanted to keep it separate from my life with Alvin, to prove to myself that my stay was only temporary; in the attic, I was a refugee keeping the Old Ways alive. Uncle Alvin didn't understand the Birthday Ritual, or What We Sing When We're Sad, or any of the other things my mother had taught me, so on all important occasions and whenever I was feeling blue, I retreated to my aerie to perform the rites. Sometimes I imagined my mom was with me all along, standing right over my should just past the point where I could see her. Sometimes I strained to try to smell her perfume.

I had a superstitious respect for the two documents that defined my last summer with Mom and Dad: The Letter and my mother's last postcard from the cruise. It said:

Darling,

One day you'll come here and see this picture in real life. I hope I'm there, too. Today your father and I are taking a little boat to a beach a local told us about. I have a blanket and the manuscript Dad bought me from that dealer on the Continent, near the ruined abbey in the picture on this card. We're going to read it in the sun, like you and I read on nice days in the backyard. I thought it would be the perfect way to open it for the first time. I can pretend that I'm with my little girl, too. We love and miss you very much.

Love,

Mom (and Dad)

Even before my adventure began, at the back of my skull lingered an instinct that the manuscript she mentioned must have been very powerful. I wondered if some of that power existed in the books my parents had left behind, and whether, if I surrounded myself with them, I could harness it to turn nostalgia into travel through time. I had no idea how much farther back these books could go.

My parents had a lot of books. I wondered sometimes if the attic floor would give out and my new Museum would be unceremoniously dumped on the old one. This lent urgency to my task.

Like other secrets, it was bound not to last, but I clung onto it with a furtive pleasure, mixed with the masochism of late-night labor in the highest, hottest portion of the house in the clinging steam of July.

Each night I tried to steady my beating heart, my furtive rattles and thumps, all of which I imagined Uncle Alvin hearing despite the story that separated the attic from the bedrooms on the second floor. I imagined he would follow the thundering of my telltale heart to the attic, and I was twelve again, sliding the misdirected letter out of my mother's tote bag, unsure of what I feared more—inciting my parents' disappointment or their amusement.

I kept my Catalogue (my toes curl slightly even now when I see that incriminating "C") in a series of composition books that I'd mined from a stack in the kitchen. Uncle Alvin bought things in bulk so he didn't have to go shopping—sometimes he wouldn't go to the grocery store for a month, sending me down the street to the 7-Eleven to get fresh milk and butter to reconstitute what we ate out of cans and boxes. I'd seen the bomb-shelter stash of composition books hiding under the little phone desk in the far corner of the kitchen for what seemed like ages. I remembered the time before they appeared as a distant era—*ah yes, those were the pre-notebook days.* It seemed to me the best way to nick something would be to take what had been ignored, unwanted, for time unknown. I didn't realize that the reverse was true in Uncle Alvin's house.

One evening late in July, after I'd snuck my twenty-third notebook to the attic for my Catalogue, Uncle Alvin came in from his evening walk around the block and said to me, "Rosie, why are you stealing my composition books?"

My telltale heart stopped beating.

I was filling my glass at the slow tap of the sink. Uncle Alvin lowered himself into a kitchen chair and looked at me with his usual deadpan expression. I could never figure out if he was serious or sardonic, or both, at any given time.

"Of course you can use them, they don't matter to me," he huffed. "My house is your house, too. So why are you making an ass of yourself pretending like you're the great cat burglar?"

I tasted the sour surge of defensiveness.

"If they're mine, why'd you just accuse me of stealing them?" I whined.

"Because you've been acting like it," he responded. "I know you've been sneaking around the house. When you act like a thief, you are a thief. Why are you trying to steal what's already yours?"

"I don't live here!" I shouted at him. I scared myself. I'm not a shouter. "I don't want to be here, and you don't want me here, so why don't we just stop pretending?"

"Where did you get that idea?" Uncle Alvin snapped. At the time I thought he was more angry than hurt. "What put that thought into your head? I feed you every night, don't I?"

I stuck my lip out and turned my face away.

"That doesn't mean you want me here. It just means you're hungry."

"Young woman," Uncle Alvin said, his voice suddenly getting low and forceful and frightening. "This is your home. I have worked for years to make it your home."

"No, it's not!" I replied. "I don't live here!"

Uncle Alvin laughed. It wasn't a funny laugh. It was a scary laugh, an angry bitter laugh.

"What do you think you've been doing here for the last three years?" he asked.

"I'm just staying! I'm just staying over until they get back."

"Playing make-believe in the attic," he snapped, and walked away.

I couldn't respond. I couldn't make myself say, "I'm just making a Catalogue so we can put everything back the way it was when they come back." I had never said that aloud, even to myself.

Instead, I sat on the floor with the water still running in the sink and my hands still wet, and I cried.

The next day, the rest of the composition books were sitting at the bottom of the attic steps. I didn't know it was a peace offering. All I saw in the gesture was the same derision he'd lathered on the words "make-believe." I didn't have a secret project Uncle Alvin didn't know about anymore. But I still had a secret, a little one I could hold in my hand. I wrote its Catalogue entry that night.

Letter.
Dimensions: 5 x 8" sheet of rag paper in 4 1/8" x 9
½" envelope.

It wasn't the only entry that I would write for The Letter. I never numbered it; instead, I gave it its own notebook, which served as well for a protective cover as chronicle, and I filled that notebook with increasingly detailed accounts of The Letter's appearance, the story of its arrival, and my mother's initial analysis of it until I felt I had nearly exhausted all possible angles on the subject, and then I resumed the attack from the original point once more, gathering up scraps of refinement and interpretation as I went along.

My electric secret. The magic letter.

CHAPTER THREE

#287: University Diploma
Dimensions: 10" x 12"
Description: Master's Degree in Literature awarded
by Columbia University to my mother. Embossed,
with embellishments in gold leaf. Status of Ph.D.
thesis: incomplete.

I WENT TO LOYOLA. I took the city bus to class every day, and afterward I took the bus back to Alvin's house, just like my two years of high school. I studied continually and made absolutely no friends.

Ignatius of Loyola was born just on the edge of the Middle Ages, in 1491, when printing was already established in the Europe and the Protestant Reformation loomed near. I read his *Spiritual Exercises* for a History of Christianity class. I was hypnotized by the language, the descriptive prompts that seemed to affirm that imagination had a place in constructing reality, that visualizing the mystical could assert its truth. After Loyola, I read all descriptions like that; I began to build my faith in history. I believed in the kingdom of the past, a place both factual and spiritual, that was composed of grains of truth in the center of foggy mountains, deep down, and the mountains that protected and obscured the truth were as sacred as what they contained.

It usually started with a name, like Bohemond. Bohemond was a name I could imagine, a name that came with characteristics, strength – it was strange, antique, infamous. I liked the name Bohemond – I liked to say it.

I liked to imagine his life – the life of a person with that name. He was christened Mark, but nicknamed Bohemond as an infant, after a mythical giant. And Bohemond, Prince of Taranto and First Crusader could endure the siege of Antioch, the agonizing winter of ceaseless skirmishing and abrasive cold, cannibalism, ambush, plots, manipulation, stagnant blood and putrefying corpses, sudden brutal violence, unassailable walls grimly showering death, hunger that made men wail and go mad, barefoot processions to beseech God's mercy, festering disease, freezing rain, the persistent and pervasive fear of Hell, darkness, and everyday butchery – but would "Mark, Prince of Taranto" really have been capable of that?

Probably not, I could only conclude; because a "Mark, Prince of Taranto" couldn't have ignited Anna Comnena's imagination the way a Bohemond would. This fourteen-year-old girl meets her father's enemy, the man who has harried his Grecian borders, in collusion with his own father, Robert Guiscard, "the sly," since before her birth. She knows all the stories of all the battles, the ingenious tactics and fearlessness and brutality of the barbarian, and she will record them later in the grand adventure story of her father the Emperor, the *Alexiad*. She devotes to Bohemond's description a level of meticulous detail that she casually denies the other crusader princes. Maybe it was because, in her mind, it had begun with his name.

He was a marvel for the eyes to behold, and his reputation was terrifying, she began. *He was so tall in stature that he overtopped the tallest by nearly one cubit, narrow in the waist and loins, with broad shoulders and a deep chest and powerful arms. And in the whole build of the body he was neither too slender nor overweighted with flesh. He had powerful hands and stood firmly on his feet.* She notes everything, with fascination – the length of his hair, short at his ears, its color and the color of his skin, the smoothness of his cheek, so closely shaved it was impossible to tell the color of his beard – the breadth of his chest and the corresponding width of his nostrils, *for by his nostrils nature had given free passage for the high spirit which bubbled up from his heart.* She chronicled the color of his eyes: blue; the sound of his laugh: a barbaric snort; the slight stoop she attributed to an inborn defect, only detectable to the minutely attentive eye.

For in the whole of his body the entire man shewed implacable and savage both in his size and glance, she sneers, but still she concludes that he is *inferior to the Emperor alone in fortune and eloquence and in other gifts of nature* – second only to her father, and suddenly I am reminded of whose biography this is supposed to be.

And my fascination with the man described becomes a fascination with the describer. In Anna Comnena's description I see not only Bohemond, but Anna watching Bohemond. I see a teenager rapt with attention, mesmerized, enthralled by the parade of character that passes before her father's throne; and by one character in particular. *He was so made in mind and body that both courage and passion reared their crests within him and both inclined to war.* And I see something similar rise within Anna.

I kept my parents' books and documents because I thought that it would make them real and whole again, the way Anna Comnena's *Alexiad* made her real. What they had left behind spoke something about them, and with calm assiduity I chronicled it all.

I made Uncle Alvin's attic the house's second Museum, and as I numbered books and arrayed the little artifacts of my parents' lives, the place began to take a shape that accommodated my presence. I started with an old kitchen table, #452 in Alvin's collection, a relic of his first apartment that had lain disassembled in the basement since he'd bought the house. I dragged it up by pieces for a workstation to organize and examine my findings. Then cushions and cabinets and an ancient wingback in a nubbly brocade (with mismatching antimacassar) that Uncle Alvin helped me hoist up on a particularly spry day. I carried the bottom. At the end Alvin huffed, "Rosie, get me a glass of water" and promptly settled into the chair, to listen, for the rest of the afternoon, while I explained the intricate shelving system I had devised for my mom's assortment of works in Greek, a language I couldn't read. I was taking Latin for the first time that year.

By the end of four years, at the age of nineteen, I knew classical Latin, medieval Latin, French, and ancient Greek. Uncle Alvin didn't seem that impressed.

"Chatterton was forging medieval documents before he was twelve," he said.

I graduated cum laude. After I received my diploma from the school president, I walked home. Uncle Alvin didn't come out in the heat. I hung my degree in my attic study, and, silently, I told mom all about it.

That summer, we legally declared my parents dead. It had been seven years since they went away. Dad's life insurance paid off my student loans and covered most of my upcoming graduate tuition. I was going to Johns Hopkins for a master's in history. It was a shorter walk.

❧

A pall hung over my first graduate term, which clung to that winter and trailed into the spring. I lurched to lecture, shuffled to seminar, and then sulked promptly home, where I sat for hours and days in the attic studying everything but what I was supposed to learn. My professors appreciated my meticulous approach but seemed put off by my reserve—I didn't like to chat, probably the result of a critical social-developmental decade spent with Uncle Alvin. But thanks to Uncle Alvin as well, I didn't really care for professors' opinions, though I was on the way to becoming one myself, by default.

And then I ended up in the Hut.

The Hutzler Reading Room houses a non-circulating branch of the university library in a soaring chamber, circular with two wings, at the back of Gilman Hall, with windows twice as tall as I was, blazoned with the crests and seals of the university's first presidents. It was also the only study area open 24/7 outside of finals period. And the only place that hosted a copy of a rare book I sorely needed for extensive and prolonged analysis.

I hadn't been aware it was possible to feel homesick when home was only five blocks away.

It was 5:00 a.m. and I felt the dawn rising in a cloud of blurry-eyed blue mist. The silence was of the intensity only experienced when you realize your comrades throughout the night have all packed up and left, and the reading room attendant has stepped out for a cigarette, and you're utterly suffocated in anxiety and solitude until mysteriously, thankfully, frightfully, someone appears from nowhere to break it.

I jumped when she began to speak; I hadn't seen her coming.

"You know why we only read male philosophers?" she asked, walking around from behind me and throwing her books down on the table across from my carefully disordered sprawl. I winced. I was speechless; while she settled into her seat at the only occupied table in the entire reading room—mine—I struggled to determine whether she was real. She answered herself when I didn't.

"It's because men sit around and philosophize," she said, cocking her head and looking up at me. "Women just get on with it. It's Max," she continued, sticking out her hand. "Short for Maxine. Comparative Lit."

Max. She was a vision of Comparative Lit. Dark hair waving lankly to her shoulders, nose pierced, she would describe her personal style to me later as "postmodern pastiche." She looked like the kind of girl that had terrified me in high school. But that terror was just a layer of my longing, the longing for that kind of girl to ask me to be her friend. I was so evolved, my desire to be rebellious had been entirely replaced by the desire to be the friend of someone rebellious.

The cursor blinked on my wreck of a paper. I gawked at Max over the top of my computer screen while she continued her one-sided dialogue.

"I mean, according to Virginia Woolf, women just needed a salary and a room of their own. But look at your friend here." She ran her fingers through the sheaves of photocopies of Abelard's works. I felt a knot forming in my throat. "Where's his girlfriend in all of this? She wrote her own philosophy in letters. Because letters describe, they communicate, like one mind speaking directly to another. Heloise's philosophy was the honesty of passion."

I swallowed hard.

"But the letters might not be real," I said.

"Real? What's real? Someone wrote them, they got written. And someone ascribed these thoughts to a woman, so that someone was probably a woman herself because, come on, what man would do that? So what's the difference?"

The difference was everything. It was monumental, it was elemental, it was fundamental, I just couldn't describe it. My consolation was that the difference lived somewhere silent and secret inside of me.

"V-vos—verit—" I was stammering with exhaustion and Max's eyebrow was shooting up. "Veritas vos liberabit," I mumbled awkwardly. I could have made it sound more intelligent if I hadn't been staring at the table while I'd searched my brain for the motto. "It's on the school seal. It means the truth will set you free."

"Funny," Max grinned. "You must have scrutinized your admissions materials closely."

That shattered my last remaining nerve. I was considering sweeping the whole mess into my backpack and marching for the exit when I darted a fleeting glance at Max's eyes and didn't encounter the glinty superiority I'd expected. Cynical and mildly amused, there was still something warm in her glance that made me feel likeable, as if she'd only make fun of her best friends that way.

"You're a serious one, aren't you?" she murmured, grinning and slapping my arm. I blushed. I'd never thought about it before, but she was right—I was very serious, solemn even. Why? It had always been the way I was.

"My parents went away and never came back," I blurted. I ventured another glance upwards. Max's grin had faded, but she didn't look bored, either. We sat quietly. I shuffled a few of my papers into a stack and set it to the side. "They had a kid, you know. Heloise had Abelard's son. They named it Astrolabe. They sent him to a monastery and never really talked about him."

I couldn't look up again.

"Who the hell names their kid Astrolabe? What jackasses," Max snorted. I felt my cheeks ache slightly and realized I was smiling too. It was funny. It was terribly funny and I couldn't stop laughing.

Max was my friend from that morning. We rarely agreed on matters academic. For Max, learning wasn't about facts, it was about style. I just longed for the moment when my education would revive the supreme sense of accomplishment I had felt the day I learned the difference between "d" and "b."

I showed Max The Letter not long after we'd met. I felt abashed, a little afraid, and a little thrilled. It came up naturally while we talked about Virginia Woolf and Heloise and the voice of ink across a page. I agreed to bring it the next day and we met, like children playing hide-and-seek, in a quiet secret place in the shadow of the library under softly shedding pine trees.

Max propped herself against a trunk and looked at my relic with a quizzical eye. She began to read the page aloud in a deep, pompous voice until I slapped her with the composition book. But I had told her the whole story, about how my mother had tutored me on it and how nothing was quite the same after that summer, and once she began to read in earnest, all the sarcasm melted from her face as it rarely did.

When she did look up, the first thing she said was, "Who is Vita?"

I was stunned into silence. Vita had always been a blank, with nothing to suggest about herself except her very neat and unslanted print handwriting. Vita had become invisible to me just the way gravity was.

"Have you ever looked for something," I asked, "you know, researched something, and gotten really frustrated until you realize that all along you just miscopied some banal little detail that turned you in the wrong direction entirely? Like, you looked for 'impalatable' when you meant 'impalpable' and suddenly you're somewhere entirely different?"

Max regarded me solemnly.

"Of course. All the time."

I slid down until my back was nestled by the long, soft, red pine brushes on the ground, and I repeated the question, which was now my own. "Who is Vita?" I asked as if Max should know, and in response her eyes flared with a random but inevitable idea.

"It's Vita Sackville-West," she said.

"What?"

"No one else could have sent this letter. It's from Vita Sackville-West."

I grunted in frustration. "Who the hell is that?" I snapped, realizing instantly that for a second I sounded like Max.

"Virginia Woolf based Orlando on her. They were lovers. You know *Orlando*, the one about the man born in the sixteenth century who dies a woman in the twentieth?"

Max told me all about her. She was rich, fabulously wealthy, from a historic family, with a labyrinthine mansion that dated back to the time when they spoke French in the English court. Seductive, swathed in publicity, drifting in the hazy world of wits and scandal-makers.

"Did they write letters?" I asked.

"Yeah, but not what you think. Virginia's pet name for her was 'donkey West.'"

"Oh." I felt slightly cheated. "Were they really in love?"

Her smile was gone, and so was the glint of humor in her eye.

"Yeah, for a while. Always, in a way. They both had their flings. Virginia, too. And it all ended pretty reasonably. They kept in touch."

Max let the letter fall to her lap.

"When Virginia drowned herself in 1941, it wasn't for love of Vita," she said.

CHAPTER FOUR

#16: 3rd Grade Biology Test
Dimensions: 8.5" x 11"
Description: Failed test, brought home to be signed;
hidden under my bed until found when moving the
mattress.

I GOT HOME that evening at about the same time as the police.

There was no squad car and there were no uniforms. There were just two middle-aged guys in brown suits in the kitchen, and Alvin said, "These men want to look at your parents' papers."

Ice water poured down my back. My face went numb as if I'd been slapped.

"Why?"

"We're investigating one of your father's former coworkers for fraud," the taller police officer said (there was a tall skinny one and a short round one, like in a silent comedy film, I noticed without smiling).

"But why now?" I asked.

"You father's personal records may contain some evidence that will cinch the guy we need," the detective explained. "In fact, we have reason to suspect they may have colluded."

I looked at Uncle Alvin. His face was grave.

"No," I said. "He's dead. Leave him alone."

"I'm sorry for your loss, ma'am, but—"

While the tall detective had been talking, the short one had been slapping at a fly that pestered him. Now with a resounding clap he had reached out to crush it with his palm on the counter and, leaning forward, bashed his head on the overhanging cabinet. The dishes rattled, the cabinet and the detective groaned, and the rest was silence while we stared.

He plowtered, which is halfway between a glower and a pout.

"Listen, we have a warrant, so if you don't let us do this the easy way, we'll just go up there anyway and do it the other way," the short one spat.

I wasn't sure I could tell the difference between the two ways or if there was possibly a third, but he was successful in communicating that I didn't actually have much choice in the matter, so I told them how to get up to the attic and then I went out to sit in the little backyard in a rusty green patio chair between ivy-crusted brick privacy walls.

I listened to the hum of cars trundling down the road and the creak of neighbors' back doors as they took out their trash. A dog barked. A child screamed with laughter. I heard the low bubble of a woman talking alone fade up and then down again as she pattered down the alley with her cell phone. I tried not to think about two men in brown suits going through my parents' stuff, my treasure trove, my sacred collection, with rough hands shuffling my mother's college books, the precious box of pictures, the fragile memories hidden in their own particular disorganization, debased by the callousness of an unsympathetic eye.

"Look, Bill, everything's got little numbers on it. Weird, huh?" I imagined the tall one saying.

"Well, I think that girl and the geeze are kinda off their rockers, Harry," I imagined the short one's reply.

I sat until the sky turned slate blue, and the shadows softened and whispered toward me. I head a car door slam and an engine rev up and grumble away. These things happened on the other side of the thick glass walls I had built around me, in the dreamland of the outside world. Inside my thick glass walls something was screaming, but I had muffled it with the big wool army blanket Mom used to put on the grass for me in the summer. The blanket had once been sturdy but it was wearing thin in places.

In the back yard, a crow called then flew onto another branch. A boom box played in the distance. My outside self got slightly damp in the evening dew.

Inside my glass walls, the screaming thing became harder to contain. When it broke through the denial I tried to smother it with, it roared things that I was afraid of. Selfish things that made me sick and filled me with shame, like "Can they arrest me for something my parents did?" Rageful things, like "Alvin is probably enjoying this. It's like he finally got back at me for ruining his life." Sad and terrified things, like "What else did they lie about? Did they even want to come back?"

A rushing sound filled my ears and I didn't know how much time went by. Eventually Uncle Alvin came out with two steaming mugs, and the sound of the back door slapping broke the glass walls around me. My outside connected with my inside and I realized that the early spring air had begun to chill subtly.

"Here." He handed me my habitual mug, thin, chipped china with a pattern of violets that reminded me of the backyard of my childhood home in spring. It used to be my mom's. Now it was full of a concoction Uncle Alvin made very occasionally on cold winter nights, a sluggish combination of scorching hot cocoa and a dollop of sweetened condensed milk.

I felt like it was some kind of subtle betrayal to accept it from him.

Alvin humphed down into the patio chair next to me with his own mug and we both looked at the ivy-crusted walls and the alley and the back of the house behind ours and above that, the sky.

"They're gone now," he said after we'd sat for a few minutes just holding our mugs, not drinking. "They shouldn't be coming back. They took a few things, but I looked at it first. Tax papers, that kind of thing. Nothing personal."

It was the most personal thing they could have taken. They took what I never knew about my parents.

"How long did you know they were coming?" I asked.

"Only definitely yesterday. But they've been intimating for several months."

"Why didn't you tell me?"

"You were finally making a little progress in your studies," he murmured. "I didn't want to distract you."

I bolted out of my chair in anger, and as I did my mother's mug slipped out of my hands and shattered on the patio.

"I can't even look at you right now!" I growled.

He said nothing.

"What is wrong with you?" I kept going. "How could you possibly think it was appropriate to keep this from me?"

Alvin sat silent as a rock.

"What do you have against me?" I said, my voice rising. "I know you didn't want me, but it's not my fault they left me here. You should have given me to someone else, someone who might have wanted me. It's always been obvious you didn't want someone else around. You never took me to do anything normal. I never made friends because of you. You pushed me through school so fast they all thought I was a freak. You never took me to the theme park or decorated for holidays or put me in the Girl Scouts or anything. I only even know about that stuff because of movies. You just wanted to talk about your books and work on your Catalogue, and I was just in the way."

The more I yelled at him, the angrier I got. I was no longer disappointed or afraid of my parents, no longer resentful of the police. All my bitterness was directed at Alvin.

Alvin wasn't a fighter, though. He had never been one for communication.

"Rosie," Uncle Alvin said softly, and I stopped because that softness made me unspeakably angry. My eyes throbbed, and I kept them fixed on the shattered remnants of my mother's mug. I heard him retreat to the kitchen. He came back with a rag and carefully collected the pieces of the mug. He stood again creakily, and I heard him shuffle toward the door.

"I don't know my parents," I said; but he was gone.

CHAPTER FIVE

#1: Spare Key to 26 Beauview Road
Dimensions: 2" x 1"
Description: They didn't know I kept it.

IN THE ETERNAL summer after my mom and I read Joe
Creekman's letter, she did everything within her ability to
feed my blossoming love of medieval adventure.
Runciman's three-volume history was one of the first
offerings. When I found the books on my bed where she'd
left them, I flipped immediately past the dedication and the
preface, like I always did when I was little, to get to the
story.

My mom had kept her thrift copies of Runciman from
college. They were smudged and flimsy paperbacks, with
plain green covers just a grade or two heavier than the
paper inside. There were no cover illustrations—just the
publisher's logo and the price, seventy-five cents.

Dusk retreated into night. I came in from the patio and
passed through Uncle Alvin's dark house. Like a ghost, I
drifted to the attic, still believing I could hide from Uncle
Alvin in his own house, a house that was actually a part of
himself.

The police had not trashed the study, not like you see in TV shows, where papers are strewn across the floor and drawers are left hanging crazily from their cabinets. There was every sign that two men had been over the place thoroughly and respectfully, and had made every effort to replace things where they belonged, even if they got a few things wrong.

I found Runciman on top of a stack of books that had previously been crowned by a 1932 Webster's Dictionary. Steven Runciman dedicated the first volume of his history of the Crusades to his mother. I picked the volume up— *The First Crusade and the Kingdom of Jerusalem*. I ran my hand across the cover, and then I held the cover to my cheek; I flipped the pages and smelled its book scent. I held it with my left hand to my left breast, the way I had clung to it awkwardly as a flat-chested twelve-year-old. I used to run across the yard with it tucked to me like that. I would swath myself in old sheets, faded and thin soft cotton with the ghosts of yellow daisies on them, and pretend I was Anna Comnena. When she wanted me for a chore, my mom would call, "Come ina, Comnena!"

I wanted a knight, a protector who could have thrown these two men in their brown suits out of Alvin's house— who could rescue my parents from the depths of the Mediterranean Sea that had swallowed them and everything I thought I knew. It wasn't a romantic fantasy. Most girls I'd known in high school seemed to want the kind of knights that gave them shining armor in little cotton-lined boxes, who could carry them away to prom and maybe write a little poetry. I wanted one of Runciman's knights— someone I could examine from my cold throne—a barbarian, an intensely flawed and kinetic being. Someone solid, irrefutable; someone breathing, heart beating, who made little creature movements to remind me he wasn't a puppet of my imagination.

If I could hold my hand to the hand of a medieval knight, and see with my eyes that he was real, I could preserve my faith in history; in the things my mother had told me when I was a girl.

My eyes burned. It was difficult to see.

I reached for the place on the table reserved for my Joe Creekman composition book. My fingers met bare tabletop and I felt a cold sliver jab between my ribs, but then I remembered I'd left it in my book bag in the kitchen when I'd come home. That felt like an afternoon spent with no one in a different lifetime.

I wanted the notebook, but I couldn't move from that place. There was a knight who was swept out of his world and into a new and unfamiliar one; he was seized by a very madness of...

My lips were convulsing. I noted the grief of my body with a numbed and detached mind. And my inner eye was driving down Beauview Drive again, the Beauview Drive that did not hold my home.

A car passed, throwing its headlamps onto the ceiling and dragging them lazily across the wall. A light like the light in the woods that day.

The dirt road had rolled out beneath us like a magic carpet whispering us through the thin air. We drove up and down, up and down, looking for Number 16. My chest tightened, my breath was short. We drove down, and then up again. I felt the bump and rustle of turning around at the end of the dirt road. "One more time," Mom said.

Each time, I saw the light in the woods. The birch woods. I saw a light; then it was gone, and I felt the passing of the light as if it were a breeze. Mom. Come back one more time.

Ignatius Loyola was studying history with me. We sat in the dim birch cloister, the cathedral above the river at Number 16, and I saw quite matter-of-factly that the light was reflected from the gilded shield of Vita's knight. "Vita left him here for you," Mom said, "But they still keep in touch."

I touched his shield. It was carved wood; I felt the pulse of the still-living tree in its grain under the gilt. I turned around to tell Loyola and Mom, but they were gone. My head whipped around to capture the knight again, but he was gone as well. With no name, he would never find his way back.

Ferns washed around my ankles. The translucent birch leaves floated above my head, as far away as the space between God and the roof of the cathedral.

The First Crusade and the Kingdom of Jerusalem slid out of my fingers and clattered onto the floor. The spell was broken and I was back in my study, reeling.

My face was wet, my eyes were dry, and I felt as if every inch of my flesh were bruised just beneath the skin. I took a shuddering gulp of air and my head spun. Physical sensation rushed back, and the calm solidity of books, the hulk of the old kitchen table, the beams of the attic ceiling that just barely rose above my head.

Where had I been? A dream, a hallucination? Was I going mad?

I felt a bit light-headed, so I reached out to grip the edge of the table while I stooped to pick up my book— when I touched it, I realized I had bent its flimsy glue spine with my grip. I buried my face in its pages and drank in the dusty musk of age, and I knew I was back—scent was the one sense that never followed me into dreams. It was time to straighten up and go to bed, I told myself; I felt the ragged fatigue of a crying jag, and I had to summon the energy to stand again.

When I rose, the knight was standing in the corner.

CHAPTER SIX

MY MOUTH HUNG OPEN, soundless. Muscles tensed, I tried not to move—as if he were a wild animal that would react to fear.

The knight stood equally still and tense in the corner opposite me, barely cloaked in darkness, but not enough to allow for the possibility of doubt. He leaned almost imperceptibly into the safety of the sloping roof beams, and I caught the ripple of a dull glint across the chain mail sheathing his arms.

The only thing to stir in the attic was the air, as a slight breeze drifted in the window, practically taunting us with its lazy gentleness, and agitated the dust that had been cast into the atmosphere by the detectives' search.

Then, without provocation, the knight barked something at me in a language I couldn't understand.

I scurried backward and stumbled over an isthmus of books on the floor. The room turned upside down with a crash. I wish I had fainted then. A bout of unconsciousness would have given my brain time to recover. As it was, events continued to unfold with baffling corporeality. The wall-builders in my brain started putting up the defenses again. I couldn't possibly be seeing him. If this were real, what else was possible? Would I be able to walk on the ceiling? Would the stars start falling out of the sky? Would my parents be waiting downstairs?

Even as I counted the possibilities with manic clarity, the wall-builders said *No. This is all an incredibly detailed mirage. What you see is nothing but light and shadow.* I remembered the night when I was sixteen and so exhausted after cataloguing in the attic that the idea that my parents' snake candelabra (Turkish, eighteenth-century) were alive gripped me like the snakes themselves. I took a nap and rolled my eyes at them the next day.

The knight moved. I heard his feet go *thump-thump* on the floor toward me, like a horror movie, and the soft rattle of his mail. Figments of light and shadow don't make noises like that. *There's an explanation for everything. There's an explanation for everything.* I tried to wedge myself against the closest bookshelf, hearing the crackle of pages as I slid over the books I had toppled.

He appeared over the edge of the table. Then he continued to walk around until he was above me, looking down.

He looked even taller from where I was. He kneeled down and peered into my face.

He was exactly as Vita had left him for me in the—what was it? A waking dream, a hallucination? A vision? What just happened? Once again my wall-builders tried to block it out. Nothing had happened. I was still asleep or dreaming. I was still downstairs on the patio. It was yesterday. Today had never happened. And at the same time, everything had happened, I was awake, and the wall-builders, faced with an insurmountable challenge, went to work trying to convince me that this was all perfectly normal. *Take a deep breath and let it wash over you. It will all be over soon.* I waited for the floor to drop under me so I could plunge sickly into the darkness until I woke up. That was how all my nightmares ended. But the floor remained solid under two booted and mail-clad feet. I noticed the knight had a sword, which is quite distressing on an unexpected houseguest.

He said something again, and I shrank. Then a genuinely cross look passed over his face and he stood. He took a few very clanky steps across the attic and repeated himself, louder. I flinched.

I started thinking that one of those poetic knights with romantic hearts wouldn't be so bad, after all.

He began to walk toward the door, and with a bolt of panic I ran to close it and leaned against it, facing him. I may have been afraid, but I couldn't let him get away. I knew I had to keep him here, to myself, and—without pausing to wonder why— a secret.

He stopped and watched me with a frustrated sneer on his face. Knights in the Bohemond mold, I decided, were far more nerve-racking than I had been led to expect. But bigger things had defied my expectations that night, most notably the fabric of time. Or my sanity. I still hadn't made up my mind.

Another car passed, and its headlights slid over the shelves and the stacks of papers and the diploma on the wall and the knight, glowing softly on his tunic and gleaming fitfully over the links of his mail. His breath caught and I saw him tense, watching the light the way kittens do when they think it's an adversary—and I actually broke into a smile.

It wasn't a dream. So the only logical conclusion was that I was crazy.

Just like that I was laughing. I was laughing at the knight in my attic. I was laughing at the smell of books and sweat and strange people that now hung heavy in the tiny space; I was laughing at myself, barricading the door against what could only be a figment of my imagination. I had actually run from him! This was worse than usual, even for me, and I was a veteran dreamer.

I laughed so hard tears ran down my face, and I was very, very thirsty and so tired I could barely stand. I pushed myself off from the door and stumbled forward a little bit, wringing my eyes with my fists. I bumped into something like a wall. With terrible certainty, I peered through my fingers and met an expanse of dingy white linen. It was breathing. I heard a low growl.

It was at that point I ran, but not without locking the attic door behind me.

❧❧

I came back with Item #352, Cousin Billy's old baseball bat.

I wondered how it would hold up against a sword. I guess that depended on the relative tangibility of the objects in question. If it was:

An imaginary knight with an imaginary sword: I would just feel silly.

A real knight with an imaginary sword: I stood a fighting chance.

An imaginary knight with a real sword: highly unlikely.

A real knight with a real sword: was uncomfortable to think about.

I rested my hand on the doorknob.

Should I get help? I wondered more than once, but my instinct persistently said *no.* I thought of who I could call. Alvin was out of the question. I didn't want him near my problems or my secrets. Max was never any help in an emergency. She was only ever good for clever commentary.

I didn't want to get the police or neighbors involved. I had to focus. I would take this thing alone, and no one was going to see me scared.

It was surprisingly easy to dwell on my personal pride while I leaned on the door preparing to confront the medieval knight in my attic, in the middle of the night, alone, with a baseball bat.

I held my breath and cracked the door open.

I stood behind it, bat wound up behind my head, ready for a homerun off a battered helmet. I saw nothing out of the ordinary in the small sliver of room that I peered into. I nudged the door open a bit more.

Moonlight and streetlight glowed on the edge of a bookshelf, the corner of the table, the flurry of papers on the floor. I saw the pile I had trampled earlier. I heard box fans humming downstairs and the shimmy of leaves outside in the breeze as it changed directions. The door creaked open the rest of the way by itself in the draft.

The knight was by the back window, wedging it open. I entered with what I hoped was a confident stride, and he looked up at me. Then he did something totally unexpected.

He bolted.

I dropped the bat and ran after him. He was clunking down the fire escape, and even though he landed in the alley before me and set off at a surprising speed for someone wearing that much metal, he still wasn't difficult to follow; he sounded like someone in a suit made of trash cans.

I dropped to the ground and he was already at the end of the block. He looked back, then swung around a parked car and hid behind it.

Unfortunately, the car he chose to slam his iron-shod body against was Mr. Edmondson's. Mr. Edmondson left his car in the alley most days and biked to work. It had an anti-theft alarm far beyond the normal level of piercing. It began to wail with gusto while the lights flashed, and almost as soon as he had crouched behind it, the knight jumped back in surprise. He looked up with equal panic and gazed down the alley, and I realized at once that he wasn't watching me, but something behind me. I turned and caught a glimpse of something brown rounding the corner at the opposite end of the block.

The knight was edging away from the car as if the machine would pounce if he made any sudden movements. Despite his earlier hauteur, it seemed that right now the thing he'd most like to be was invisible.

Luckily, due to a few well-placed remarks by neighbors, Mr. Edmondson was aware of how disruptive his car alarm was. He had given me a spare key to the car to turn it off in case something triggered it during the day, since either myself or Uncle Alvin were almost always in the house. I still had my keys in my pocket from earlier that day, so I went forward to silence the beast.

With relief, I realized no one had peeked their head out into the alley to see what the commotion was. They were all used to the alarm anyway.

I looked to the knight. He had stopped running, from me anyway. But I had vainly hoped for a little respect or some healthy awe—after all, I had just slain the metal dragon, right? Instead, he curled his lip and straightened his shoulders defiantly. He strode toward me and landed a victorious kick on the car's rear bumper.

Of course, he wasn't expecting that to re-trigger the alarm. This time, however, he took the offensive and unsheathed his sword and put out the demon's taillights.

That woke up the neighbors.

The knight wound up for another blow with a mighty roar when I rushed him and grabbed desperately at his arm. He actually lifted me off the ground slightly, but he didn't follow through on his second strike.

I saw a light go on in Mr. Edmondson's house. I tugged plaintively on the knight's arm, but he was still determined to dominate the car. A neighbor's dog was barking, and I heard a back door open a few houses down. I did the only thing I could think of to draw the knight away from the scene. I snatched his helmet off his head and ran like hell.

It worked. In ten seconds flat he was sprinting after me amidst a cacophony of squeaks and clinks. I rounded our garden wall and he slid in behind me just as I heard Mr. Edmondson's back door slap. The knight, heedless, launched over me to retrieve his helmet, and I reached up to slap a hand over his mouth, signaling him to be silent and still.

Down the alley, I heard Mr. Edmonson's groan as he surveyed the damage to his car. He hollered a few times, asking if anyone was there, but it wasn't the kind of request that most vandals eagerly respond to, so he probably did it just to blow off steam. I held my breath, imagining any slight sound would bring him screaming down the alley toward me as if I had hoisted up a neon sign proclaiming "Yes, she's guilty!"

After a little pacing and grumbling, Mr. Edmondson thumped back into his house. Slowly, I eased my grip on the knight. As soon as I let up a little, he shoved my arms from him and plucked his helmet from the ground, planting it firmly on his head. He began to get up noisily, and I put up my hand to hold him back once more. He shook me off roughly again, but he also straightened up more stealthily.

The fire escape was too loud to climb back up without attracting attention, so I tried the back door. It was unlocked—exactly as I had left it when I came in heartbroken, so much earlier that night that it felt like another century—before the Middle Ages had begun.

We crept into the living room and up the stairs. I said a little prayer of thanks that Uncle Alvin slept like the dead. I hadn't even seen his curtains stir during the commotion with the car outside.

So I led the knight by the hand up the endless creaking staircase back to the attic. It was the best place I could think to put him. It was where I kept all my other antiques.

I was so relieved to be between its safe beams that I didn't even remember I had left Mr. Edmondson's keys where I dropped them next to his car.

CHAPTER SEVEN

#45: Atlas of Legendary Places
Dimensions: 11" x 9"
Description: A book entirely about places that don't
  exist, given to me by my parents.

THE RELIEF ONLY lasted one fleeting minute. Then I was facing a sweaty, tall, real knight in my attic, and I didn't know what to do with him. He didn't seem to know what to do with himself, either. In a clear attempt to assume an air of authority, he strode heavily to the window and looked out with squinted eyes. A drop of perspiration fell from his temple to the windowsill with a pathetic "pop."

Just a little while ago I'd thought my life was collapsing as I found out my parents and Alvin had kept secrets from me. Now time itself had been turned upside down, and all the things that had happened before felt like a dream.

I took a deep breath and tried to organize my thoughts. Now that I had him installed once more in my attic, I had to find a way to communicate with him. It was clear he didn't understand English, new or old. I tried catching his attention by proclaiming "Welcome to my home" in Latin. He shot me a look of incredulity. He clearly wasn't expecting me to know Latin. I asked him his name. He didn't respond. Clearly he didn't understand Latin, either.

I tried French. This time he curled his lip and turned back to the window. He didn't know French, either, and didn't like people who did. I tried Greek, just for the hell of it. Who was I kidding? He wasn't going to know ancient Greek.

Regardless of our language barrier, there was one question I knew what I had to ask him, even if it meant clownishly acting it out to him. Here came our "me Tarzan, you Jane" moment.

"What's your name?" I asked, this time in plain English, pointing to him and then myself extravagantly. Really, the monkey business was insulting my aesthetic instinct.

He didn't respond, at least not in words. He just looked back from the window at me, as if I were a pest interrupting important business.

I pointed at myself and said my name slowly, with repeated jabs of my finger to my sternum. *Me Rooooosiiiieee...*

He just sniffed, tossed his chin up, and then ignored me once again. Oh, sure—now he knew my name, but he didn't see any reason to condescend to tell me his. I went up to him, tugged his elbow, pointed to myself, and said my name one more time. He shook me off, grunted, and pointed to his tunic. There I saw a lion regent in a field of daisies d'or. Oh, right. That explained it. *Don't you know my family, peasant?*

He straightened his shoulders and declared, in a commanding tone,

"Joachim Kriegmann."

You could have knocked me over with a feather. Was he Joe Creekman? They had no conceivable connection except dubiously similar names—and the letter itself. I couldn't shake the superstitious feeling that crept into the back of my mind. Despite the eerie consonance, I still had to consider the possibility that Joe Creekman was someone else entirely.

Joachim seemed pleased with my awe and turned fully to me, as if expecting me to bow to him. I was about to do no such thing. But when he turned to me, I saw more clearly the sweat pouring down his face, and his armor made such a clamor even with that little gesture that I was suddenly very eager to encourage him to take it off. He didn't creep about the place so much as clink, and even if I hadn't been trying to hide him from my uncle and the man whose car he had trashed, it would just get a little annoying.

I wasn't sure how to communicate. For a tense few moments, I stood in front of him, uncomfortably close, but still afraid to approach him, remembering his earlier distaste for being handled in a demanding way. It was time for me to swallow my pride. The only way I could get him to comply would be to give him the respect he wanted. I stooped down on one knee and lowered my head to him. Then I stood up again and pointed at myself and my loose, light clothes. I was wearing one of my dad's old plaid shirts rolled loosely up to the elbows, and I billowed it out to make a fanning motion. I wasn't the most outstanding example of modern fashion sense, but it was enough to get the point across: *Would you like to take your portable oven off?*

He seemed pleased with my deference, and he held out his right hand, wrist up. I saw a leather strap that held his mail sleeve and glove together. Now I understood, and it made such perfect sense that I felt guilty for not recognizing it earlier—he had remained in his cumbersome armor because it was too difficult to remove it alone.

When I untied it, the mail glove clunked to the floor and I gasped. I picked it up quickly, as if doing so would reverse the sound, and I was surprised by its heaviness; it was still warm. I slid my own hand into it and flexed my fingers, but winced when the links pinched the tiny hairs on the back of my hand. It was too large for me.

I set the glove on a shelf dominated by loose papers and added the next glove to it. I was still tense, expecting him to rebuff me haughtily at any moment, but instead he reached up and took off his helmet, then pulled back the mail hood underneath it. His hair was plastered to his head. He handed me the helmet while he unbuckled his sword belt. Like a trained butler, I placed the helmet with great respect on the shelf, but I flinched a little when he held out his belt and sword, as if I were afraid the sword would bite me if I touched it. I didn't know where it had come from or what it was made of or what it could do. But worse still, a tiny little voice in my head whined, *Don't be ridiculous*, as if it hadn't gotten the memo that there was a knight in my attic.

The knight didn't react patiently to my hesitation. He shoved the belt into my hands with a frown and I nearly dropped it. I felt prickled at being used so harshly, but I had no way of communicating it to the knight except by crossing my arms and frowning back (after I'd set his sword neatly by his other accoutrements).

It was the first time I'd had a chance to look at his face clearly, without the helmet, in the bright moonlight streaming through the windows, and my crossness was replaced with curiosity. He must have been struck the same way because he withstood my silent examination with an even temper.

It was hard to tell his age, but I thought he could be around eighteen; he didn't seem very mature in attitude, but his face was weathered beyond his years. If I looked closely, I saw the vague beginnings of lines from the corners of his eyes, as if he were used to squinting. His lips were chapped and colorless, and long but gently shaped.

In the light I saw more distinctly the color of his eyes. It was a muddle of shades of gray the way some people's eyes are shades of blue or brown, impossible to pin down to one dominant strain; they weren't glinty, but opaque like aging steel.

I also saw the residue of his journey through my imagination on his way to the attic. On his tunic was a faint but certain pattern of large yellow daisies.

"I used to play dress-up in sheets like that," I told him. The grating sound of a language he didn't understand snapped him out of our mutual daze. He lifted his arms brusquely, and I realized that the complaisance during his undressing that I had taken for granted was the result of being used to the attention of a squire or valet.

As I removed the rest of his outer, protective garments, his movements anticipated me a little, prompting me to the next strap or buckle. Next came the long heavy outer tunic (yes, those were daisies, I noted with close examination until he stomped his foot impatiently) and the pieces of mail underneath, the hood and the chin pieces that would have tied to the nose protector of his helmet. And under that, a kind of leather waistcoat that laced together; I loosened and lifted it off of him as he turned, his arms outstretched. I scrunched my nose as he released a distinctively medieval scent.

At long last I had pinched and worried the last straps, and he stood in shirt and leggings. I felt a slight wave of relief—guiltily—that he still looked knight-ish even without the armor. Maybe I was afraid that, if he stopped looking like a knight, I would be forced to acknowledge what he really was—a complete stranger—and then I would truly begin to be afraid. But without all the bulky metal hung around him, he looked a little reduced—leaner and younger too.

"You need a glass of water," I said to his uncomprehending ears. "Stay here." To make my point, I pushed his shoulders, backing him into the ancient wingchair in the corner. He scowled, refusing to sit, but he didn't follow me out, either. When I left, with one more backward glance I locked the door behind me.

I was getting water for the knight. And after I had touched him, smelled him, heard him, helped him out of his armor and out of trouble, it all felt a bit eerily normal already. The kitchen grounded me again—the warm orange halo cast by the overhead light was familiar, and the glasses in the cabinet and the sound of water running in the sink made me feel like it was any other night when I was savoring the lateness alone with my books.

As I climbed back up the stairs, my exhaustion caught up once again, even while I longed to continue to puzzle over the knight. My mind struggled against it, but my body was already cranking down for sleep. I couldn't fight it physically— my eyes drooped, my head was sore. I felt like I was walking through water, and my head was weighted with all the questions I still had to ask.

But it looked like I had a reprieve before further investigation. When I reached the attic, the knight was already asleep in the wingchair. He'd had a rough day too. After traveling through time and dreams, reality can fall on you like a ton of bricks. I put the glass of water on the floor by his feet. Then I did what I had done often in the last four and a half years—I gathered all the cushions and beanbags and quilts that had accumulated gradually in my attic, and I piled them into a bed that I crept onto with a sigh of relief, a pile of my favorite books within easy reach.

As I drifted to sleep, I thought of the hospitality traditionally offered to pilgrims in stories of chivalry. When I had thought of Anna Comnena earlier that night and wished for a real flawed and human knight, I hadn't anticipated on getting one; and when one arrived, I found it much less frightening to view him through the lens of fantasy.

✌✍

The next morning, the knight was still there.

I wondered if he would stay, and, if so, how many more mornings I would think to myself, *He's still there*, with that curious mixture of relief and anxiety; or how soon he would become part of the scenery. Even that morning, I could imagine getting used to hiding a knight in my attic; maybe it was because of the fleeting second last night when I saw my own curiosity in his eye.

I rose shakily from my cocoon of cushions and saw him there clearly in the matter-of-fact morning light, kneeling in front of the window. He had spent the night in a chair, and now he was down on his knees, back unforgivingly straight—and I had slept on a heap of cushions and still felt bruised and groggy.

I thought he was praying at first, but I noticed on a second glance that he was actually peering suspiciously out the window. I remembered the figure I had seen last night and suspected that he didn't stay with me in the attic all night because I kept him in, but because something else made him afraid to appear outside.

I stood, and it felt more like the rest of the world was plummeting down from underneath me. I glanced at the glass of water that I had brought for the knight, but it was empty. I lurched out the door, clumsily locking it behind me, and stumbled to the bathroom on the next floor, where I washed my face, drank six Dixie cups of water, and unexpectedly threw up.

I felt much better and made my way down to the kitchen. I guess I'd have to feed the knight too—if my morning vertigo was a combination of exhaustion, anxiety from the previous night, and the process of bridging centuries with my mind, the knight couldn't be feeling all too well himself. I saw the broken shards of my mother's mug in the trash when I emptied the coffee grounds into it.

I scrambled some eggs lazily and stared at the spring leaves nodding outside the kitchen window. Outside, cars trundled to work and a gaggle of preteens ran by in plaid uniforms. How strange.

I grabbed some toast, scooped the eggs onto a big dinner plate, poured two cups of coffee, and— remembering a little late the supposed secrecy of my operation—tiptoed back toward the stairs. As I put my foot on the first stair, I heard Uncle Alvin down the hall in the living room.

"Rosie?"

I stopped as if caught in the act of burglary. Uncle Alvin was in his recliner, across from Aunt Patti's old chair, rubbing his eyes.

I nearly dropped everything, but I managed to make it into the living room and set my dishes on the coffee table. My heart stopped when I realized he'd notice I was carrying two coffee mugs. But he removed my anxiety by assuming one of them was for him and reached forward for it. In the morning light, he looked frailer than I'd ever seen him. His face was gray and his hands shook a little; he set the coffee quickly down again.

"When'd you come in?" he asked.

I searched my mind.

"About one or two," I said.

He looked at my clothes.

"Sleep in your study?"

"Yeah. I was reading."

Alvin cleared his throat wetly. For a second I was afraid he was choking, but it subsided, and he patted his mouth with a handkerchief.

"So was I," he said and reached for the nearest volume, *Paleolithic Site of the Douara Cave and Paleography of Palmyra Basin in Syria: 1984 Excavations*. He began to read, and he picked up the coffee again with a slightly steadier hand. I stood and began to gather the rest of the breakfast things.

"Maybe I'll walk with you to class today," Alvin said as I prepared to leave. "It's been a long time since I've been on the Hopkins campus. It's beautiful in the spring, if you think that kind of thing is useful for learning."

"I wasn't going to go down to school today," I said on my way out. "Seminar was canceled." For me, anyway.

I was almost out again when Alvin arrested me at the door with another remark.

"I was woken by Mr. Edmondson this morning," he said. "He came and knocked on the back door."

"Oh." I thought my voice was too squeaky, so I tried to lower it a little as I followed with "What did he want?"

"Someone vandalized his car last night. Did you hear anything?"

"No," I answered quickly. I added, "I went out like a light last night."

"Well, Mr. Edmondson dropped off these," he replied, picking up my key ring from the table next to him.

Acid panic flooded my skull. I struggled not to turn pale.

"Oh," I squawked again, "I must have dropped them on my way home yesterday."

"He found them under his car," Alvin continued.

"Maybe someone kicked them there," I reasoned. "It could have been whoever did that thing to his car."

"Smashed the tail lights in," Uncle Alvin informed me, but I was already running up the stairs.

❧

When I got back to the attic, the first thing that I noticed was the overwhelming smell of sweat, the dank heaviness of the air that comes in early summer after multiple people sleep in a small room with poor ventilation. It was already getting warm, but hopefully in May it wouldn't yet reach sweltering.

The knight was standing by the window. I elbowed a few books over on the table, sending some crashing to the floor, and set the now-lukewarm plate down, sat back in my desk chair, and sipped my mug of coffee. I didn't have any to offer him, but that didn't stop me. He probably didn't know what coffee was anyway, I muttered to myself.

The knight looked at me as if I were a peon barging into his fortress of solitude unbeckoned, but today I wouldn't let that faze me and I waved him to the table. I cleared an old kitchen chair of its colony of books and pulled it up for him. With a slowness that indicated his importance, he strode forward quickly, and standing, scooped a heap of eggs onto a piece of toast with his fingers, and stuffed it in his mouth.

I was about to nudge him when some kind of respect stopped me. I coughed gently instead and handed him a fork. He looked at it briefly, set it down, and then repeated his grab-and-stuff method. I didn't want to think about what might be under his fingernails. I picked up my own fork and tucked in. He glanced up at me, and a swift look of disgust danced across his face before the curtain of impassivity fell once more. Of course.

I'd have to housetrain my warrior. I started to understand how the Byzantines had felt.

He loaded up another piece of toast and carried it to his armchair in the corner, where he ate loudly enough to wake the neighborhood and then licked his fingers. He could eat like that, but he wouldn't share a table with a peasant.

I didn't have any books on the care and keeping of a medieval knight. He hadn't tried to speak to me since the night before, but that morning I was simply thankful he waited quietly for me and responded to my prompts with a minimum of indignant resistance.

After breakfast, I began to collect the dishes upstairs, thinking of my next step. As difficult as it was going to be, I had to show him the washroom.

Thankfully, Uncle Alvin didn't venture all the way up to the Museum level frequently these days, unless he had sent me up first with a few cratefuls of newly catalogued exhibits. So it wasn't difficult to sneak the knight down one floor to the nearest bathroom, where I intended to introduce him to modern standards of cleanliness. It wasn't a task I savored, but I knew it must be done, so I undertook it like the most stolid of charitable workers.

First I showed him the light switches. He seemed slightly stunned at the sudden appearance of light but not at all impressed with my role in it. I realized he didn't understand the connection between the switch I flipped on the wall and the light that turned on yards away. So I showed him how it worked. He turned the light on and off with a satisfied air, but after I showed him, he wouldn't let me work the switch. Instead, he batted my hand away as if it were unworthy. So much for sharing.

Next I turned on a faucet. I wasn't expecting much this time, but he surprised me again, launching himself on the water with undisguised glee. I left the tap on lukewarm, and he splashed his face and neck, then cupped handfuls of water onto his hair, giving it a vigorous scrub. Then, while he was still dripping, he ducked down and drank the water straight from the faucet. He straightened up, snatched the nearest towel and patted himself dry. I took that opportunity to reach over and turn the water off again, and it was the first time he acknowledged my presence since I'd turned it on. He cast me a condescending scowl, and then, turning back to the mirror, he began to primp.

He arranged his hair, which was loosely curled now, so it framed his face like a Greek sculpture. It was roughly jaw-length, and he finger-combed the ends to make them even. He even patted down his eyebrows. He picked his teeth with a long pinkie nail. Then, to my utter disgust, he plunged his index finger into his ear, fished around for a while, and then wiped it on his legging.

Next I showed him the toilet. It was awkward.

Finally, I completed our tour with the shower. I stood outside the curtain and turned it on. I took down a bottle of shampoo and squeezed some into my hand, holding it out for him to smell. Then, on a playful impulse, I reached up swiftly and pulled his head down into the stream of water, slathering the shampoo into his hair. With an angry grunt, he snapped back, shedding drops of water like a wet dog, and he retaliated by shoving me bodily into the shower's stream.

I scrambled to shut the water off, and stepped out again with as much dignity that a fully-dressed and completely soaked person can have.

"We are done here," I stated. Leading him by the elbow, I took the knight back up to the attic, where I deposited him and scooped up the breakfast things. I thought it was time to give him a little personal space. The truth was, I didn't want to think any more about everything I still had to teach him. Just in case, I locked the door behind me.

❧❧

Downstairs, Alvin was on the patio reading Ovid to the geraniums. When I'd been younger, I'd always stopped to listen when Alvin recited the classics—it was how I got such good marks in Latin class, though after a while the teacher pivoted from impressed to concerned at my aptitude for speaking a dead language.

Watching Alvin read reminded me—the way things do inevitably in warm spring light—of the last day of school six years ago, when I had come home with the heavy regret that I always felt at the end of the school year after watching my classmates pass around their yearbooks and seeing my teachers clear off their desks and become real people with the glimmer of personal lives. Alvin had been on the patio then too, when the daffodils along the edge of our tiny yard were just fading as the irises awoke—we only kept flowers that didn't need much care—and he had been reading the *Ecologues* aloud mostly for the pleasure of hearing the words roll off each other.

Now his voice just made me angry and uncomfortable.

I remember once, when I was little, I was complaining after a boring visit from Uncle Alvin, and my mom told me to be patient with him because he was a very unhappy person. I didn't understand what that meant; we had a happy family, wasn't that enough? My mom's remonstration to be kind to him had the opposite effect, making me slightly awed and afraid of him.

His wife Patti had died only a few years into their marriage, two months after her doctor found a tumor in her ovary. I couldn't understand his grief; she was the aunt I'd never known. If old school pictures tell a story, he had never been an ebullient person to begin with, and eight years after his loss, when I was born, he had become a virtual recluse. My mother always seemed at a loss, despite her overflowing good intentions, for how to help him.

So, she invited him to stay at her new house in Harford County and help take care of the baby. To her surprise (even more to my father's) he accepted, and Alvin arrived in his black sweater in the middle of June to do everything he could to make motherhood easier on the sister who had longed for it her entire adult life. For the hectic first months of my life, he was a fixture in our home, helping with the cleaning, soothing me when my mom was exhausted, cooking dinner, and playing on the battered upright piano in the living room. According to my mom, he took care of me as tenderly as if I were his own kid. They made him my godfather.

When I arrived at his house at the age of twelve, originally for a three-week stay, I was vaguely terrified of him. I couldn't remember much of his early visit, and since then I had never perceived the tenderness my parents described; just an imposing gravity that made me afraid to speak too loud when he was in the house. Gradually I warmed up to him, I think because that summer, after my parents vanished, I began to understand what made him the way he was.

I wondered if the knight upstairs had left behind a pair of anguished parents when he disappeared from their time. I wondered if my parents had been shunted back to his era in some kind of exchange, and the seven intervening years had just been a fluke.

Uncle Alvin was reading the story of Cadmus today, while the flowers in the garden bobbed, looking for the seeds they'd sewn last year.

I didn't notice I was watching him until he turned. He looked directly at me and actually stopped in the middle of a line. I didn't smile or say anything, I just darted back down the hall and up the stairs to the attic. I told myself I couldn't leave the knight alone too long.

In the attic, the knight was once again peering out the window, this time with more open curiosity, taking in everything of the neighborhood he could see from the one small square opening.

I joined him there, and when I looked down I saw that Alvin had stopped reciting and now sat in a patio chair, head bowed over his book. I couldn't tell if he was reading or napping. He looked crumpled from here.

CHAPTER EIGHT

#762. Knight.
Dimensions: 6' 1", 160 lbs.
Description: Medieval knight transported by hallucinatory daydream. Gray eyes, signs of premature aging. Distinguishing markings: crest of lion regent in field of daisies d'or. Occasional expostulations, currently uncategorized Germanic. Illiterate. Doesn't like Latin-speakers. Or the French. Or women. Or peasants. Or mussing his hair. Or losing his helmet.

THE KNIGHT WAS SHINING. Along with the grime he had cleaned from his hands and face, some of the weariness was gone too, while the muted colors of his clothes made his skin look fresh, and the morning light made him look young and solid.

"How did you get here?" I had to ask aloud. I thought I knew: he had traveled out of the story I'd read as a child and out of my mind like Athena popping out of Zeus's forehead.

I thought of another angle, one that might be more useful. I pulled out an atlas and opened it to Europe.

"Where are you from?" I asked. To make myself clear, I pointed at the map, and then to him. He stepped forward with the air of someone who heartily enjoys stepping forward authoritatively to a map. But his sense of authority plummeted from there.

He didn't recognize specific places because the map was too accurate. It wasn't how he was used to seeing the world on a page, which would have happened rarely anyway. I remembered that most medieval maps had Jerusalem at their center, and the rest of the known lands squished eccentrically around it, fading off into locations like Eden or the realm of Prester John.

Then I remembered the medieval encyclopedia my mom had bought for me the week after the letter arrived. Contrary to the title, it wasn't an actual encyclopedia from the medieval era, but a fat hardcover indexing fun facts and pictures about the Middle Ages for children ages 8–12. I had held on to it, like everything else, because I couldn't bear to part with these artifacts of my childhood. I pulled it down now and opened it to the chapter on cartography. Sure enough, there was a fold-out reproduction of a medieval map with Jerusalem at its center.

This time, there was a glimmer of comprehension. I wondered if he had been shown a similar map once, while his father pointed out the general area of their castle; on a map of this scale and inaccuracy, a fingerprint that probably covered several counties. I could see from the delight in his eyes his recognition and awareness of the honor of being able to identify his home on a map. With a triumphant string of words I still couldn't understand, he jabbed at the map's middle-left quadrant—roughly northeastern Germany.

For my undergraduate degree, history majors were presented with the choice of learning French or German as their modern language requirement. I had chosen French.

It wasn't worth feeling bitter about, though, since the German that Joachim spoke was probably very different from the modern language. But at least I had somewhere to start.

I raced to my bedroom, dug furiously through the detritus under my bed (pink glitter-gel sandals still waiting to be worn when I got home and could run around in my own backyard again) and fished out my laptop. I rushed it back upstairs and started cross-listing Germanic languages with the approximate date that I could guess the knight had come from using his armor as a clue.

While I typed busily in the search engine, the knight walked up behind me. He shook my shoulder roughly and said a few words. I looked up, peeved that he would interrupt me while I was doing important work. He peered at the screen, then, not comprehending it, he seemed to take no interest in it. It was covered with words he couldn't understand, anyway, and he had no way of knowing the power contained in that little piece of unremarkable gray material.

Soon I was so absorbed in my search that I lost sense of my surroundings, the time, and my increasingly bored and impatient guest. I'm not sure how long I had been happily navigating the web for materials on the languages of medieval Germany, but I was drawn out of that world abruptly by his hand shaking my shoulder again.

I squirmed away from under his hand, shooting an annoyed glance up at the knight, and he responded by batting the computer off the table. I watched, numb and paralyzed with shock, as it landed on its side and then clattered to the ground, upside down. The CD drive was poking out crazily, and a silence filled the attic as it clicked off.

I wanted to scream, but there was no way of making him understand just how much damage he had done, much less making him care. He had wanted my attention, and now he had it. Ignoring my dumb rage, he gestured toward his mouth. It was lunchtime.

Furious, I picked up my computer and stormed out of the room, locking the door behind me yet again. He didn't try to stop me—he probably thought I was rushing off to do his bidding. I was more eager than ever to learn his language now so I could give him a piece of my mind.

I plugged in my computer in my bedroom and tried turning it on. It whirred a few times, and the screen blinked, but it was clearly feeble. I put it to rest gently among my cushions (mismatched, faded) as if that would make it heal itself, and then I headed downstairs. I would have to finish my research at the library. Then figure out a way to explain to Uncle Alvin why I needed a new computer.

I ran into the kitchen to pick up my book bag and found Uncle Alvin there eating a sandwich. He watched impassively as I gathered my things.

"Where are you going?" he grunted through a mouthful of rye bread.

"School," I replied, rooting in my bag to make sure I had a notepad and several pens as well as my student ID.

"I thought you didn't have class today," he muttered.

"Independent project," I replied, and hurried toward the door. He called after me before I could get out.

"Don't forget your keys," he said. I had. I sprinted back to the living room to get them from the table where he had placed them this morning, like a courtroom exhibit, and then I left through the back door without yelling goodbye.

I had had enough experience interpreting Alvin's many-colored silences to know that he sensed I had clearly brushed him off earlier when I told him I wouldn't be going to campus. I wanted to get out of that house.

Immersion in the library helped me overcome my conflicting emotions. Three hours later, I felt a little less nasty toward Joachim (after all, he didn't know what he did), and I had virtually forgotten Uncle Alvin. I took advantage of the computer lab to do some more online work, but with information this arcane, my best sources were the books themselves. I left the library with an armful in addition to the volumes bursting from my bag. For a second, I thought I'd left my student ID inside, and I turned around, slamming into the person who had been shuffling out the doors behind me.

"I'm so sorry!" I shrieked before I realized it was Max.

"Easy there, tiger," she said. I hadn't seen her since the afternoon before … *before*. Would it be more accurate to say it was before the police or before the knight—which marked the beginning of the ineffable span of history that had passed since yesterday? I realized I had spent an entire day without wishing she were there to keep me company. I felt guilty. The thought floated through my mind that despite her bravado I was her only friend.

"Where have you been hiding?" she asked me.

"Nowhere. My uncle's house. I haven't been hiding," I said.

"I didn't see you in seminar," Max pouted, tilting her chin down at me. The Gilded Lily: Text Analysis 1215 to 1275 AD was the one class we shared through an interdisciplinary fluke of the comparative literature and history departments. I had skipped it that day. "Was wondering if you'd caught the plague."

"No, just the plaque. Between brushing," I joked mirthlessly, trying to sound casual.

"Class oppression?" she prompted.

"Um, no, not work," I blushed, unable to lie.

"So, secret romance?" Max continued, her typical smirk crawling up her face.

"Nothing, just research," I mumbled. "Life of the mind sort of thing."

"Research, but not for class?" Max countered.

"Class is just a distraction," I squeaked. "I have to go now. I need things at home."

"I thought you were going back in?"

"No," I said, feeling my pockets and finding my ID in a back one. "That was just a feint."

Max looked more than amused at my discomfort, but I was eager to escape. I didn't want her distracting me from my mission. I set off at a brisk pace, hoping to shake her. Max could beat even my best attempts at self-discipline and denial, however, and she trailed me easily.

"I'll walk with you," she said. "It's so nice out today."

It was; the quad was scattered with lounging clusters of undergraduates in the shade of the bordering trees. One large circle appeared to be an Italian class. Later in the afternoon, a dozen or so students would probably gather on the upper quad near Gilman Hall to play cricket—it seemed to be the habitual cricket spot, presumably because the lawn was the perfect size.

We swerved toward the tiered marble stairs that separated the upper quad from the lower. They were dusted with yellow pollen and the juvenile leaf shoots that had blown down in the swirling spring winds. I looked at Max, whose eyes drifted around the spring scene, muddy patches of green and the bright white steps, carried into the moment.

I was afraid to share Joachim with Max, perhaps because it meant I would have to share Max too.

"So how's life," Max asked, trailing her hand into a boxwood and then smelling her fingers.

"Okay. You know." I said. "The usual."

"Come on. If you haven't been engaged in a secret experiment that requires six dozen books, you should at least make something up."

I made something up.

"You're going to have to try better than that," Max replied. "I know you know nothing about glassmaking. And you're allergic to ... that other thing."

I sighed.

"Alright. Uncle Alvin just wanted me to look up a few things for him, for the Catalogue," I said, and I felt a pang of shame. "What have you been up to?" I asked weakly, trying to divert attention.

"Nothing at all. The truth is, I don't exist when you're not around," Max quipped. I rolled my eyes.

We marched on. I wondered why I had to start the conversation; Max was usually full of useful non sequiturs for moments like these. Every second of tense silence was one second closer to blurting.

"So ... the flowers are nice," I tried, as we descended the steps behind Hodson Hall, toward dim, curling San Martin Drive. The edge of wooded Wyman Park bristled up on our right side, dark and scruffy like an unshaved cheek. The knight would have to learn how to shave, I remembered; he probably had someone do it for him in his family's manor. I'd teach him the safety razor this afternoon.

Max wasn't interested in the flowers anymore, so we strolled to the house in (mostly) companionable silence.

"Here we are," I said as we wended up a slight hill off a narrow grassy dog park. "Chateau du Me."

"Thank God," Max moaned. "I need a glass of water."

I paused with my hand on the door. I guess she could come in briefly; there had to be a way to get her out again. As much as I enjoyed Max's company, I had never had the urge to bring her back to the house with me. In the back of my mind, I think I was afraid she would dissipate like a mist when she crossed the threshold.

We came in the front door instead of taking the shortcut down the alley and through the garden. I still wanted to avoid Uncle Alvin, and he spent more time in the living room in the back of the house than anywhere else. The front door opened onto the hall, and to the immediate left we entered the kitchen. Max traipsed in after me as if she'd lived here all her life. She threw herself down in a seat by the table and picked up the note that was there.

"'Rosie—GPL 'til 5—A,'" she read. "Is this some kind of anagram? Are you looking for the Holy Grail?"

"What?"

I crossed over to her.

"Let me translate," I said, taking the note from her and folding it while I explained. "'Rosie, I'll be at the George Peabody Library until 5pm today, signed your Uncle Alvin.'"

"Rosie?"

"Yeah, my uncle calls me that sometimes. For Rosie the Riveter. Old joke." I reflected for a second. "Sort of. It's not really funny, is it?"

"You know where the name Rosie really comes from, don't you?"

I knew that whatever I guessed would probably be wrong.

"The flower?" I ventured.

"No. Why would I ask you if it was that obvious?" she snapped. I had to admit, she had a point. She continued,

"It's existed since the Middle Ages, and it kinda fell out of use for a while, and then when the Victorians brought it into vogue, they probably did it because of the flower. But way back when, it was the Old German word for 'horse.'"

I felt a swift stab of adrenaline—my heart skipped as if, by talking casually about medieval etymology, Max would discover that I was hiding a primary source. Incriminatingly, *A Concise Dictionary of Old High German* peeked out of my bag on a spare chair, as if it wanted to make a point of not being consulted sooner.

"So I'm a horse," I objected. "Ugh, Max."

"No, think about it," she continued, smirk expanding "What's a knight without his horse?"

I couldn't believe it.

"You know what," I said, "just quit it. It's not funny."

"I'm not joking! Seriously, a horse gives him nobility and mobility—it's a companion, a natural navigator—allows him to marshal respect—carries him and is always loyal—"

"Are you sure you aren't mixing horses up with dogs?"

"Maybe a little, but you get my point. I'm not a details person."

"Yeah, well, you don't go around calling girls horses," I whimpered. "Or dogs for that matter."

"Why not? They're noble creatures. Just ask any knight," she replied.

It was almost as if she knew and was just playing with me.

"Listen, I have work to do," I said.

"No you don't," Max countered. "You're just going to go up to your attic and stare at your parents' stuff."

I wheeled on her.

"That is not all I do," I growled. I wasn't sure if I was offended because it was untrue now, or because it had been very true until recently. "I have lots of things to do."

In the angry silence that hung over the few seconds that followed, I heard an enormous sneeze from upstairs.

"I thought your uncle was out," Max whispered.

"It's an old house and it gets creaky," I covered. *Oh God*, I thought, *can you really hear that much from down here? What kind of house* sneezes?

Max's teeth glinted as she leaned toward me.

"No, it really is secret romance," she grinned, and began to get out of her chair. I moved to the threshold between the kitchen and the hallway to the stairs and tried to block it.

"There's no one. I mean nothing," I said.

"Oooh, what were you going to do? Read Erasmus to each other?" Max clutched her heart and threw her eyes up to the ceiling. "*Oh, I just love him*," she sang, "*It's so sexy when he corrects my Latin.*"

I've already tried Latin, I thought. Max stamped past me and was already making for the stairs. I ran after her, steaming. But trying to stop her was like trying to grasp fumes.

"Max, what is your problem?" I screeched. "This is *my* house! Get back here!"

Max looked down at me with an inkling of sympathy, as if this weren't my house at all.

"If there isn't anyone up there, why don't you want me to look?" she taunted. Her persistence was beginning to feel mean-spirited. And all the while we kept climbing higher—I thought if she were bound to meet the knight, I should at least make sure it was on my terms. Finally I pulled her aside, into the third-story Museum.

"Listen, I've been keeping a secret," I said.

"I love your secrets!" Max replied, hoisting herself onto a wooden countertop and swinging her legs. Instantly, she softened—I realized this is what she had really wanted, not to violate my secret, but to be let in on it voluntarily.

"You know the letter I showed you yesterday?"

"Vita Sackville-West telegraphs surreal message of divine justice and naughty knight," she chirped.

"Well, yes. Except the Sackville-West part. I'm pretty sure you made that up."

"Whatever. It's in."

"Well," I continued, "That night, some detectives came to look at my parents' stuff, and I think I had some kind of a breakdown."

"Wait, wait—why did detectives want to look at your parents' stuff?" Max inquired, leaning forward. I cringed.

"Something my dad might have been involved with," I said. "It's not important. They're probably wrong anyway. But ... I wasn't happy about it. And I went into this daze. And I saw things, in my head. Like a dream, a really vivid daydream. Things from the story, and my mom, and Vita, and ..." I didn't want to tell her about the forest I had seen as a child. I was afraid she would try to go there too. "And when I snapped out of it, something got left behind."

"Like what?" Max asked.

"Like a knight," I said. "Actually, definitely a knight."

"What do you mean?" Max said.

"Exactly what I said. I looked up and the knight from the story was in my study."

"How do you know?"

"He looked like a knight. He sounded like a knight. He ... smelled like a medieval knight." As I spoke, I heard steps above, very slight creaks, as if someone were trying to move without making much noise. I was a little flattered— Joachim must have finally taken my lead, I thought to myself—it wasn't his usual stomp. Max heard too, and her eyes widened as she looked from the ceiling back to me.

"So he's for real." Max said. "Someone who genuinely ran around with a tin pot on his head."

"Yes."

"And he's in your attic now?"

"Yes."

"And he has some kind of dust allergy."

"Apparently."

"Is that it?" she asked, sliding off the cabinet. "Why didn't you tell me sooner?"

"How do you do tell someone, 'I'm hiding a medieval knight in my attic'?" I asked her.

"Is he armed?" she responded, with a curiously excited glimmer.

"Yeah. He has a big sword and all that. Don't stare," I muttered.

"I'll try not to," Max grinned, and before I knew what I was doing I was leading her up to the attic door.

I pushed the door open slowly. From the dim stairwell, the widening sliver of attic looked golden, as if there were no shadows, as if the walls themselves shed light. Stepping up into it, as my eyes adjusted, I noticed the hints of darkness again, hiding in the slender spaces between bookshelves and in nooks. It was almost idyllic, as if the attic itself had evolved from that perfect birch woods.

That perfect empty birch woods. The knight was gone.

"On a scale of one to Zelda," Max said into the vacuum of my disbelief, "how mental was your breakdown?"

"He was here," I said. "I left him here. Why would he go away?"

"Hmm, let's see, because you imprisoned him in your attic?" Max said.

"Damnit, and I forgot to feed him!" I declared angrily.

"That also may have been a contributing factor to his urge to escape," Max replied.

"He must have climbed down the fire escape. That's how he got out last time," I remarked, walking up to the open window. "Look, I helped him out of his armor and put it here." I pointed to the shelf where I had so carefully set out his gear. It was empty now. I bent down to run my hand along it, looking for any indentation or sign that could prove to Max—and myself—that last night's and this morning's events had been real.

I couldn't meet her eye. I hung my head in disappointment, and that's how I noticed the footprint on the floor. Joachim must have stepped in a spot of engine grease in the alley, because across a few spilled papers on the floor was a footprint unlike those made by any shoe in our house: large, treadless, with round indentations for nails.

I was about to beckon Max over to take a look at the evidence when I heard another loud sneeze behind me.

Max never sneezed.

I whirled around. The sneeze had come from the monk hiding in the corner behind the door.

As soon as I saw him he bolted for the open window with a thin wail. I stared, gaping, but Max's shouts of *"Get 'im! Get 'im!"* mobilized me, and I launched myself after him with an agility I didn't know I had. I tackled him just before the window, and he struggled fitfully but soon gave up once I had bodily pinned him to the floor. Close inspection revealed him to be just as much a monk as Joachim was a knight: a leather-sandaled, brown-robed, tonsured monk.

"What do I do now?!" I asked.

"Interrogate him!" Max commanded.

"Who are you?!" I screamed in his face, carried away by Max's gusto. The monk shrank from me, scrunching his eyes closed.

"What are you doing here? What is going on?" I kept shouting, and I felt a strange frustration grow inside of me as I did. "Seriously, where are you all coming from? Is there a door I left open? What are you doing here? What do you want with me? Why did you pick me? Are there more coming? Don't you know how to knock before you come in?" I didn't notice when I started shaking his shoulders, but I shook him so hard his head bobbed limply back and forth. "Why are you nodding? What are you trying to say to me? Are you trying to say something to me?"

"You're shaking him," Max pointed out, and I stopped. I stopped roughhousing him altogether and I stopped shouting, and it was then that I finally heard his voice. He had been murmuring the whole time in a trembling voice, in the same language the knight had used that was incomprehensible to me, but soon all he emitted were squeaks of distress.

"Calm down," I tried telling him more soothingly. "Just calm down and talk to me."

But he was clearly past the point of helping, and even as I spoke to him more gently, he worked himself up into a higher pitch of hysteria.

Then I had a brainwave: if he was a cleric, then he theoretically should be able to speak Latin.

"Who are you?" I asked in Latin.

I couldn't tell if he understood me that time, because with a final gurgle of anxiety he fainted away in my arms. Well, under them.

"What are you going to do with the body?" Max asked casually.

CHAPTER NINE

#125: First Aid Kit
Dimensions: 5" x 3" x 1"
Description: Small metal case containing bandages,
*   pain reliever; closed by a complicated childproof*
*   latch that is impossible to figure out when*
*   panicking during an emergency*

I IGNORED MAX and tried to prop up the monk's head as gently as I could while I fanned him with a nearby book. In situations of real need, Max was truly useless.

The monk's eyes fluttered open, and when he saw me he looked for a second like he was about to faint again. He squeezed his eyes shut, and when he reopened them a look of profound fear and disappointment settled on his face, as if he had been fervently hoping he would find himself somewhere else.

"Shh, I won't hurt you," I told him in English. Then I repeated myself in Latin.

I sighed, set his head down on a cushion that I fished from a pile behind me, and sat back.

He really ought to have a glass of water, but I didn't like to leave him like that, and Max couldn't be depended on to take care of anything. I'd just have to be quick. I didn't think he was going anywhere.

"Wait here," I told him in Latin. "I'll get you something to drink."

I ran down to the third-floor bathroom and back up as quickly as I could with a toothbrush cup full of water. I gave it to the monk in small sips until he looked less pale. Meanwhile, I got a good look at him. I estimated he was about my age or a few years older, but he looked both older and younger than Joachim in some ways. His face was more mature and he didn't have the gangly look of adolescence, but his features were less weathered. He had dark rings around his eyes that were set off by the paleness of his fainting spell. The eyes themselves were a plain brown, like his hair; he was about my height (thus significantly shorter than the knight) and less strikingly handsome than Joachim as well, with an open, round face that would be more pleasant if it weren't subterraneanly pale.

"Who are you?" I asked in Latin, as gently as possible.

"My name is Adelbert Lufthild Baldfunke," he replied, his voice high with nervousness.

"Do you have a nickname?" Max asked sarcastically. She said it in English, even though I knew she understood Latin as fluently as I did—we had had conversations in it. Adelbert didn't even register Max's presence, however; he was wrapped in self-consciousness and fear, and he only saw me, the girl who had until recently been sitting on his chest.

"What are you doing here?" I asked quietly.

He burst into tears.

"I don't know," he said. "I don't know. I'm sorry, I'm sorry, I'm sorry." He trailed off again into his Germanic tongue. I sighed. I didn't know what else to do to comfort him, so I just let his anxiety run its course. I handed him a tissue which he used vigorously, and in a few minutes he had calmed down and even sat up a little.

"Where are you from?" I asked him.

"Saint Vitus' Abbey by the county of Faeglenod, fief of the Sire of Bisongarrd, vassal to the Holy Roman Emperor," he recited. Saying it seemed to soothe him further, as if the sounds of the familiar places made them slightly closer. "I'm a monk."

"I noticed," I said encouragingly. It hit me that he must have been the brown shape disappearing around the corner last night. "I see you seem to be in pursuit of a knight. Can you tell me where he went?"

"Pursuit? *Pursuit?!*" the monk squealed indignantly at me. "I don't even know why he runs from me. But for the second time he has escaped me."

Me too, I thought. I wondered how I would respond if someone had asked me why *I* felt so strongly about capturing the knight and keeping him to myself.

"Well ... why are you running after him?" I asked Adelbert.

That's when he told me the whole story of his transferal to my time, a story that brought the evening I had spent with my mother poring over the letter back to vivid life. I listened raptly.

"I was working in the scriptorium after compline, when all the brothers but those chosen to measure the vigil were meant to be in bed," he began. "That was my first sin. It was motivated by pride, for I longed to look over the page I had written that day, and ambition, for I hoped to continue to add to it and thus indulge the insatiable desire I had to embellish my tale and add to the length of my works.

"My task was to record the miraculous events incurred by the relic of our patron saint housed in our sacred vault. I had collected many stories of curious events, but none were enough to quench my thirst for pure novelty, a shameful pastime that overtook the sacred duty of veneration that was meant to be the purpose of my travail.

"As my collection grew, I began to augment it with a few inventions of my own. Each had a grain of truth at its center. The one I was working on that evening was inspired by a spook tale a novice had narrated to me the night I arrived at our abbey years before. It concerned a knight who had visited the abbey a mere month before my arrival. He was a boisterous fellow and not liked by the brothers. The day he left our abbey was the last day he was heard from in all the county. Many ascribed it to the brigands in the area, but a few suspected a more eerie fate."

My spine began to tingle.

"I didn't get many details from the novice that night, and later he denied knowledge of the tale. But I yearned to spin the story and make it my own. So I sat down that night years later in the scriptorium after compline to a secret journal I had kept to myself for ten whole years, since the first time my fancy had ever directed me to record the visions of my imagination. And I wrote about a vicious knight who abused his hosts and faced the judgment of our patron saint. After an hour of strenuous invention, my wrist began to ache and I put down the pen to relieve it. All of a sudden I was overcome by a blinding light like the one I had described in the fiction with which I had just profaned our saint's memory, and I found myself in this room, last night."

Adelbert took a long and shuddering breath. With the recitation of his story over, the power that storytelling had given him drained out of his face, and once again he was a very frightened young man.

I felt more than a little scared myself. I realized that before me sat the author of the tale that had awed me as a child, the story that had dominated my imagination for seven years. I felt a little like I was in the presence of a rock star. His story about the power of books also made me think, with a tremor, of my mother's last postcard and the book that she said she had been about to read on the day she and my father disappeared.

"It was lies that got me into this trouble," he sighed pathetically. "I am always making things up. That's why my brethren call me Bullaficta in mockery of my secular name, Baldfunke."

Bullaficta in Latin meant, roughly, "imaginary blister."

The pejorative ignited the leave-no-author-behind comparative literature spirit in Max, and she piped up for the first time in Adelbert's interview.

"In these parts, we respect people with a good sense of invention," she proclaimed. "I propose we give you a new nickname. Something that shows off your creative spirit with pride." She glanced at the stack of books beside her and snatched the top one. "From now on, you're not Bullaficta. You're Bulfinch."

She handed him the copy of Bulfinch's Mythology, but he was still far too wrapped up in his own worry to examine it, and he let it drop from his hand limply.

I thought I'd try another tactic and draw more of the story out of him.

"So last night," I said, "You were behind me as I chased the knight? He was actually running from you?"

"I can only conclude the same, since he later returned with you, but I have no idea why he fears me," he wailed. "The moment I arrived in this house and saw him there, though I've never seen him before in my life, I recognized him the way it is said in stories a father can recognize his long-lost son. I knew he was the knight in the story I had written, and I also knew that the only just way to repent for my sin was to hear the true end of his story from himself. But he eludes me!" he cried dramatically, grasping his hair in frustration.

"I know the feeling," I said, thinking of my parents. "We can look for him together."

"Hey, don't leave me out of this," Max interjected.

I looked up at the window and out at the declining light of the day. My head swam a little.

"It's getting late to go looking now," I said. "We can search for him outside tomorrow. I'll take you around the neighborhood. He can't have gotten far," I said, as much to reassure myself as Adelbert. "We can take a walk in the morning."

Max groaned. "The morning? That's a little before my breakfast time," she muttered to me. I ignored her.

"For now, let's eat and rest," I said to Adelbert. "You could use a little of both. Wait here while I get some things."

I left the monk in the attic in relative confidence. I didn't even lock the door behind me. He had seemed so real— even more real than Joachim seemed to me by then.

Max followed me down to the kitchen.

"So, what are you going to do with him?" she asked me confidentially.

"What do you mean, what am I going to do with him?"

"Are you going to take him to the news? Experts? I don't know, sell him on eBay?"

She reminded me of the movies I'd watched when I was little, when well-meaning children had to hide a fairy, mermaid, or alien from the grown-ups, or else it would be kidnapped by Science. Was this why I still dreaded letting anyone else know about my visitors? I imagined a futuristic Society for the Protection of Time-Displaced People using me as an example of historic mistreatment.

"I want to help him," I said. And then, after a little thought, "I want to get to know him."

Max contemplated for a moment.

"In the biblical sense?" she asked.

"No! Max, I'm being serious!"

"Hey, I just wanted to know if the field is clear. You know I'd never steal from a friend."

"Don't get any ideas."

Unfortunately, Max was entirely composed of ideas. It was probably why she got so little done.

"Sometimes I feel like my brain is a TV and I'm flipping between *King Arthur* and *Bridget Jones's Diary*," Max sighed.

"You boggle me. Boggle. I don't know where it comes from."

"Oh, you know."

"This isn't a game of dress-up," I admonished her. "They're real people and they need me."

"Oh yeah? That knight who ran away from you, him too?" Max countered.

"He doesn't know what he's getting into," I replied shrilly. "He's headstrong and he doesn't know how this world works."

"Well, tell me this. When you take that armor off him, does he still look like a knight?"

I was silent.

"Then it's all dress-up to me," Max concluded. "And as long as it's all the same, I'm still calling the monk Bulfinch."

"You can't just give him a pet name like a dog," I objected. "It's completely undignified."

"And Adelbert is a byword of respectability in our century?" Max queried. "Anyway, I don't care what you do, I'm calling him Bulfinch."

I heard Bulfinch sneeze upstairs again, and I made a mental note to bring him an antihistamine tomorrow.

CHAPTER TEN

#476: College Acceptance Letter
Dimensions: 8.5" x 11"
Description: Packet saved in box, "To Show to Mom
when She Gets Back"

AFTER I GOT Max out of my hair, I put together a tray of food to bring up to my new friend. The task was pleasanter than when I'd been caring for the more prickly knight.

I was still trying to understand what he meant in the grand scheme of things: the puzzle of time travel and how it fit in with the story I'd read in childhood. When I was young, I'd believed in the story, precisely the way Bulfinch ... Adelbert had described it. I wondered if I was the only person in history who had ever taken him that seriously. Maybe this is what had enabled me to be their channel into my time.

I assumed that my imagination was the device that had brought them here. I just wished they thought I was that important, too.

I hurried up to Bulfinch, eager for more conversation.

"When did you join the order?" I asked after we had eaten. I found that asking him questions about home comforted him and calmed him down.

"I joined the abbey when I was seventeen," he said. "I was much older than the other novices. I am a younger son, but my father was prosperous and allowed me to remain in his household though I showed no interest in knighthood. In those days, I had total freedom to read and study as I pleased." He sighed. "I had a tutor as a child, but my mother was afraid I wasn't spending enough time in manly sports, and sent him away when I was an adolescent. The truth was, I was too smart for him by the age of fourteen." Bulfinch beamed. "I traveled to the nearby cities every year to collect more books and to visit libraries. I taught myself languages and even ..." he lowered his voice, "read the philosophy of the Saracens and their beautiful poetry. But my study was limited. I longed to learn more."

As I listened, I could see his world as he described it to me.

"The summer I was preparing to travel to the University of Paris, my father died unexpectedly in a riding accident. My oldest brother took lordship of our small fief and had very different ideas about how the family resources were to be spent. He would not support my journey to Paris and I had no money of my own; it was far too long and perilous a trip to take without my family's help.

"It was then that my brother informed me," he swallowed, "that he had dedicated me to the Church. Of course I was infuriated. He was treating me like an infant— a parent offers his newborn son as a promise to the Church, but a brother does not offer his grown brother simply as a ploy to get him out of the house. Of course, I had to obey, or risk damnation for my entire family, including my poor dear mother. So I was exiled to the obscure abbey of St. Vitus, where I hoped that by my outstanding scholarship I would attract the attention of a donor who would one day send me to Paris."

I imagined Bulfinch letting the monotony of every day lull his senses, letting his imagination emerge and dominate.

The afternoon was deepening into evening. I didn't think to listen for Uncle Alvin's return. In the attic, we were safe from the whole world. I had brought enough food and drink to satisfy us, and then to graze on later. I gave Bulfinch a brief tour of the third-floor Museum, but we soon returned upstairs. We agreed to spend the rest of the night upstairs, to watch in case Joachim returned by the fire escape.

In the attic, I began to explain to Bulfinch gently about life in modern Baltimore. He lapped up the information eagerly, but he stopped me often to tell me about his own home, so the going was slow. Sometimes he told little dramas and comedies about daily life; sometimes he just interrupted with a remark, like "Brother Aefle would love that. He's my only friend."

I found the best way to describe modern life to him was through literature. I told him a history of his future. Bulfinch was delighted by all the books in the attic. Before I could make it as far as Daniel Defoe, we were sidetracked. He was fascinated with the printing press, with cheap identical copies of a single book. He loved to hear about the explosion of prose fiction in the writing world. In his time, poetry and song were the most popular means of storytelling. When he was excited, his ears would twitch and I could almost imagine his hair standing up a little on end.

I showed him glossy photos, reproductions of art in museum books, mass market paperbacks, and bound photocopies from class. His joy in books was contagious.

And his enthusiasm for learning drew out memories of my mother, until I was telling him the story of my childhood and my parents' disappearance.

I didn't tell him about the Letter yet, or the events of the night that had precipitated his and Joachim's arrival in my world. I wanted to keep things simple. I wanted to feel free, relaxed. I wanted to enjoy my new friend.

We coasted into comfortable silence while we reclined on the cushions on the floor and watched the sky darken into night. The lights of passing cars began their shifting dance across the walls. Bulfinch asked what the lights were, and I explained cars. It wasn't as difficult as I expected; he wasn't mystified at all, but seemed eager to know more about how they worked than I could tell him. *Thank goodness I won't have to explain computers right away*, I thought, remembering my broken laptop downstairs.

We went to the front window and I pointed down at the cars parked along the street while we waited for the next car to pass so we could watch together as it came closer, released its specter in our room, and trundled away. He watched with a happy grin on his face.

I ran to the window on the other side of the attic, overlooking the back, pried it open, and climbed out onto the fire escape, which I used to creep up onto the roof. Bulfinch followed. We settled our backs against the chimney and looked up at the two or three stars we could see through the aurora of city light. We listened to the boom-boom of distant traffic, the hum of cicadas, and the conversation of neighbors muffled by a curtain of damp spring air. A plane flew overhead. An Indian dance song blared from the open windows of a car that sped by a block away. Each new sound triggered an awed and eager look from Bulfinch.

We were suspended on a thread, and I tried not to move or breathe too deeply in case it snapped and dropped us back into time. But for that evening, surrounded by the sounds of night and springtime, with the silent company of a friend, I felt that if I stayed up here long enough I'd be able to feel happiness physically, like raindrops in my hand.

CHAPTER ELEVEN

#73: Dress-Up Bin
Dimensions: 5' x 2' x 3'
Description: All children's sizes. Not much fun anymore.

WE STILL HAD a cranky knight to go hunting for.

In the morning, I crept downstairs by myself to reconnoiter and gather breakfast supplies. On the kitchen table, I found the same note Uncle Alvin had left yesterday, but now there was a coffee stain on it—signs of life. A wave of relief and guilt washed over me. I wondered if I would have noticed if something had happened to him yesterday and he hadn't come home. But the days were getting warmer and in the warm weather Alvin spent most of his time at the Peabody Library, which was air-conditioned (unlike the house, where we only had window units in our bedrooms, and only after Uncle Alvin's doctor recommended them).

I was filling the tea kettle when Max appeared in the kitchen window, making me jump. My mind had been so occupied with other things, I hadn't expected her. But she snuck up on me, like she always did in quiet moments.

"Hagiography is my favorite word today," she said through the window above the sink. Then she walked around to the lower, larger window by the table, opened the screen, and let herself in.

"Hagiography," I repeated.

"Yeah. It just sounds so, you know, so ..." Max settled herself into a kitchen chair as casually as if she had walked in the front door. "It's good to say. You know what else I like? Erstwhile. We don't use erstwhile nearly enough."

"What does erstwhile really mean?"

"I dunno. Erstwhile. While the erst."

That morning, I just wasn't interested in Max's loopiness. My mind was full of Bulfinch and Joachim. I opened the fridge and fished around for eggs.

"Why aren't you paying attention to me?" Max whined.

"I'm tired," I said. "I couldn't sleep until almost dawn, and then I drifted awake early this morning." I'd never had a job to break my habit of rising late. But today, I'd opened my eyes at 7:00 a.m., buzzing with a new energy and anticipation. I lingered in bed, trying to sleep again out of habit, but I'd felt as if twelve cups of coffee had been poured directly into my veins.

"Your mind is wandering again," Max noted.

It always is when you're around, I thought.

"I'm going to take Bulfinch for a walk today," I said. "We're going to look for the knight."

"That's what quests are about," Max replied. "Wandering. Nay, wending." She watched me as I rooted in the fridge and pantry, searching for breakfast food in vain. All I found were a box of stale Cheerios, three almonds in a jar, and a lump of ancient Velveeta.

"Are you going to take Bulfinch out as is?" Max asked. "You might attract some stares, with the robes and all that."

Last night, Bulfinch and I had been so wrapped up in conversation that I hadn't stopped to consider how strange his clothes looked.

"I don't have anything for him to wear," I said. "I don't think he'd have anything on under those robes that would look less funny than the robes themselves ..."

"So. Steal some of Alvin's. No big deal."

"No. I'll take the bus to the mall today. Guestimate the size, bring a few things back."

"Come on, it'll take too long, and you've got to get knight-hunting. Think of poor Bulfinch cooped up there with nothing to do and Joachim wandering the streets, penniless and alone ..." Max's simper was insincere, but the thought was convincing enough.

"Okay," I said, feeling a thrill as I made the decision. "Hey, wanna come with?" I asked Max.

"Sure," Max huffed. "I'll bring the leash." I rolled my eyes. I couldn't tell if she was being sarcastic about the leash or about coming at all.

I hoped Max would come and hoped she wouldn't at the same time. I wanted to show off my newfound friendship with Bulfinch, but I didn't want to share him.

"We'll leave in about an hour," I said. "Look out for us."

I bounded up the stairs with a light heart, even though I still hadn't found breakfast. We were going to start our adventure. Bulfinch was going to see the world. Starting with Hampden. And I'd be coming too.

❧

Uncle Alvin's house was a nirvana for any five-year-old looking to play dress-up, but it wasn't the best place to equip a medieval monk to go incognito in the real world. Unless I wanted Bulfinch to look like a 1940s gangster (and, at best, he'd probably only pass as a low-level mob accountant), most of the Museum's collection of discarded clothes was out of the question. Even though it would only be a slight improvement, I had to sneak into Uncle Alvin's personal wardrobe.

The results were grim. Uncle Alvin was an inch taller than Bulfinch, but about fifty pounds heavier. Bulfinch looked like a scarecrow in the khaki shorts and lurid pink Hawaiian shirt that I knew wouldn't be missed from Uncle Alvin's closet.

A pair of deteriorating Birkenstocks and an Orioles baseball cap (to cover his tonsure) completed the outfit.

Overall, Bulfinch looked just about as goofy and absentminded as he had in his Benedictine robes.

Outside, Max wasn't waiting, so we left without her.

Bulfinch didn't seem all too bothered by what I had made him wear. I wondered if he'd change his mind when he saw what other people on the street were wearing, but he seemed to be habitually oblivious to his looks. I took him out the back door, into the alley. I thought it would be a good place to start: alleys, parks, and other places where Joachim might have found some limited shelter during the night.

"What clues could we find that would lead us to him?" I wondered aloud.

"Remember he attacked that vehicle down the street?" Bulfinch prompted. "Perhaps he has continued to display his confusion through violence. I suggest we look and ask around for other incidences of petty destruction."

It was a logical idea, but it had to make me laugh.

"Bulfinch, exactly how big were these cities that you visited for your collection of books?" I asked him. "Trying to track him by looking for vandalism would be like following a trail of breadcrumbs the morning after a storm that rained bread."

We trekked in silence for a few moments while I reflected that I didn't have any better ideas to offer. We walked another block. With a completely different tone, Bulfinch pointed to a narrow patch of weeds between two houses and said,

"That's where I slept the first night." I imagined how terrifying the ordeal must have been for him, those first twenty-four hours knowing no one, having no shelter or guide. No explanations, only fear.

"What did you do that day?" I asked him cautiously. It was the one part of his adventure he had seemed reluctant to talk about yesterday.

"As I said, when I saw the knight, I knew instinctively he was the villain of my tale," he said. "I chased after him, but when the automobile began to scream, I became frightened and fled from it. I watched as you subdued it and guided the knight back into your home. As the whole world was strange and new to me, I could not understand whether you were a force for good or evil, so I kept my distance, waiting for a moment when I could espy the knight alone and approach him without the interference of another party.

"I felt very alone in this grim and friendless place," he said sorrowfully. "I longed to communicate with another person, but I feared the consequences. After trembling in shadows and corners, watching the strange vehicles, and hearing the unfamiliar and inexplicable sounds of this city, I squeezed myself into that little passage and slept, fitfully. I woke once to find a rat nibbling at the hem of my robe."

I shuddered.

"The next morning, I cautiously made my way back to your house, and waited in the shadow of the shed across the way. I watched your uppermost window, waiting for a sign of the knight. I must have fallen asleep from the exhaustion of the previous evening, for when I awoke later and cautiously mounted the ladder to that window, the knight was already gone. The room was empty, so I entered to see what clues I might find there or evidence that the knight would return. Then I heard you stir on the staircase inside, but you were already too close for me to flee, so I hid and hoped you would leave again soon." He paused. "You must remember the rest, of course."

By that time we had walked several blocks, and I realized that we had barely been paying attention to our surroundings while we were immersed in talk. We were never going to find the knight this way.

My stomach growled, and as if on cue Bulfinch's whined in response. We laughed.

"Let me take you to a store where we can buy some breakfast," I said, "and then we'll have more energy to look for the knight." It made perfect sense, even if it gave us the excuse to dawdle longer.

I took Bulfinch to the 7-Eleven, where he watched the hot dog rollers with obvious delight. We bought hot dogs, chicken fingers, fries, donuts, and Slurpies. We took them outside and sat on a retaining wall in the shade to eat. Bulfinch laughed, looking at his Slurpie, saying he had never seen something so blue, much less imbibed it. He asked me if cultivators had really developed a blue raspberry and did its juice really have such an overpoweringly sweet taste, so different from everything else in nature?

If Bulfinch's senses were sharpened to the freshness and modernity of my world, his presence drew my attention to its more medieval aspects. While we were in the store, my eye fell on the papers while the cashier rang up our food.

Suddenly the words "Chronicle" and "Times" in their titles had new meaning to me.

While we ate, I asked Bulfinch what crimes or sins the knight had been accused of, according to the story the novice had told him years ago.

"He was a very vain and unchivalrous man," Bulfinch replied as hotly as if the knight's offenses had been directed at him personally. "He taunted the poor, the weak, and the young, and he mocked those older, wiser, and better-read than he. He spent hours preening himself in the mirror and then flicked pebbles out his window onto the bald, pious heads of the novices below him. He was said to be of generous means, but he donated little and was rumored to have tried to steal the candlesticks from his room.

"While his prowess in battle was still untested, he had a reputation for cruel treatment of servants and ungallant behavior. I have no doubt—rather, the novice who narrated the tale to me had no doubt—that he would have become a monster had he grown to maturity and inherited his father's estate."

"He didn't seem that bad when I met him," I contemplated. "Just a little spoiled."

"Well, I only tell you what was passed to me in confidence," Bulfinch countered quickly. "He is still but a young man, and I am sure that he understands enough of the rules of decency to prevent him from being a threat to you in your home."

We let the topic go. I watched as Bulfinch discovered all the ordinary details that had become invisible to my eyes— the grills of the gates over the narrow passages between houses and the initials smeared into the sidewalk when the pavement had still been wet, the way tree roots formed ridges and broke through the concrete and the houses that seemed so spindly and so tall. His ears twitched until I thought they would drop off, and there was a spring in his step that reminded me of a five-year-old unable to contain his glee.

I was glad to see him revived and happy. I was glad simply to be able to feel glad for someone else.

We ambled down the hill and crossed the street, following a track worn in the grass of the dog park. I saw women toting young children out of cars—the lower grades that finished earlier must be getting home now. They squirmed and the mothers looked stressed-out, but from the other side of the street they looked idyllic. Ahead, a scruffy teen mowed a lawn—it must be the first mow of the year. We pottered up from the trail onto the sidewalk just as the kid with the lawn mower turned, the chute of his machine pointing toward us, coughing exhaust and a flurry of clippings. We scampered through the dust, and then I paused under the next tree, inhaling the sweet scent of cut grass. Bulfinch stopped a few paces beyond me and succumbed to a three-minute fit of sneezing.

When he recovered, he looked back at the lawn mower with a grin on his face.

"Interesting," he said, while he watched it trundle up and down the lawn, "how soon your time is becoming customary to me. I no longer fear these strange things." He paused. "It's as if there are so many new things that, rather than become overwhelmed by them all individually, I've already accepted them as a whole."

But crossing streets, I still had to hold him back with a hand on his arm to keep him from rushing headlong into traffic whose speed he didn't understand.

I wondered how I would have fared if our situations had been reversed, and I was dumped unceremoniously in the calamitous, dirty, poorly lit Middle Ages. I depended entirely on my petty habits and tics for well-being. I liked things to be complete and orderly, even if my order made no sense to anyone else. I would probably be the nun who snuck into the scriptorium after hours to make sure everyone's pens were parallel with the edges of their desks.

We strolled down the avenue, past bright shops, one that sold only shoes and chocolate, another stocked with comic books and plastic statues of smoking bunnies, and further down, when it got seedier, a sex shop glittered around the corner, the corsets in its window cheap and gaudy in the plain sunshine. A cat ran out of an alley. A woman with a heavily lined face and smeared makeup sat on her stoop smoking and grunted at us as we walked by. I tried to see it the way Bulfinch might.

His gaze drifted happily everywhere. He asked about my education, about the university, and so I turned our steps in that direction. After all, Wyman Park and the campus were plausible places for Joachim to be hiding out, with lots of benches and nooks.

As we made our way up shady San Martin Drive, he finally asked about the evening that he and Joachim had arrived. I still hadn't shared my half of the story. Something about the solemn presence of the trees reminded me of the forest of my dream, and the atmosphere seemed to inspire Bulfinch as well.

"How did our appearance affect you?" he asked. "Surely the shock must have been great."

"I'd already had a shock that night," I said. "In fact, I think that may have played a part in the miracle. I don't think you appeared in my attic by coincidence ..."

I explained the old misdirected letter to him, the page from his uncompleted story. I skimmed quickly over the alleged scandal involving my parents and finished with his and Joachim's materialization.

Bulfinch overflowed with pride and enthusiasm.

"My story was really potent enough to perform a miracle?" he gushed. "Imagine that! The story *I* wrote was enough to send two men through time! My portrait was so vivid it *came alive!* Think about how many places I could go if every reader was so moved by my prose that they drew me into their world—how much I'd learn!"

I'd never thought of it that way. All along I thought it had been *my* imagination, not Bulfinch's, that had done the trick. Maybe it was both working together.

"... my story was reprinted in a *book*, *hundreds* of years later!" he was still exclaiming. "I must be *very* important!" He was bursting at the seams.

Now I had no choice but to puncture his bubble just a little, for the sake of our investigation.

"Actually, I'm really sorry to say this, but I've looked very hard for the book that page came from," I told him, "And for seven years, I've come up with nothing."

His face fell so tragically that I had to cheer him up somehow.

"You certainly were important enough to translate and preserve!" I reminded him brightly. "Possibly as recently as my century. It's just that, well, you're a bit difficult to find." Then it hit me. "But now I know something I didn't before. We can look up your abbey. Maybe there are some records available about the monastery's library collection."

I doubled our pace and soon we emerged into the campus. I barely gave Bulfinch time to admire it (and the buildings were beautiful and classical and warm between the pink riot of the flowering trees) as I swept us toward the library.

The Milton S. Eisenhower Library's five subterranean levels were packed with wild-eyed pre-med undergraduates, angst-laden thesis candidates, and other indigenous species of scholar. The crowded confusion made it easy for

Bulfinch to slip in through the gate directly behind me, with no form of ID of his own to check in.

Unfortunately, this meant every public-access computer station was occupied. We had to wait in line to use a standing-room-only computer that was intended for catalog use, in the deepest level of the library.

All the while, Bulfinch finally displayed some of the righteous disapproval of modernity that I had been expecting all along.

"This is the library?" he kept repeating. "This is the *library?*"

I had thought visiting the library would have been the high point of his day. I fought the urge to respond, *No, this is just the room where they keep all the books.*

"Where is their respect for the books?" he muttered. "Where is their respect for the knowledge?"

I prickled a little at his snobbery.

"The knowledge here is for everyone," I said. "They're using the library the way it was designed: as a tool."

"But the tool can be made beautiful as well," he continued, without looking directly at me. His eyes were slightly glazed, taking in the harsh fluorescent lights, the steel shelves, the gray carpeting. "We make the tool beautiful because we respect the good it does. And that respect helps us use it better."

Virginia Woolf's Oxbridge and Fernham came to mind, and I silently agreed with him.

It was our turn at the computer, and I hurried up. As I opened the web browser and began typing, I tried to explain the internet to Bulfinch succinctly.

"I'm looking this up in a kind of big book that everyone in the world shares," I told him. "Anyone can put something in it. It's stored remotely in things called 'servers' and you can use one of these to access it. A computer's like a librarian getting your book down for you."

As I scrolled through the results (there were a lot of St. Vitus' Abbeys, and the most famous generated the first few pages of hits), Bulfinch simply glanced at the screen and said, "If anyone can contribute, then how do you know that what you read there is true?"

I dropped my hands from the keyboard and stared him straight in the eye.

"Bulfinch, you already understand the internet better than most people I know," I said.

I turned my attention back to the results, and after a little more digging (and a few more people collected behind us in line for the computer station), I found Bulfinch's St. Vitus'.

I read the article twice, checking the date and its references. Then I logged off and pulled Bulfinch aside to an undisturbed corner near the stairwell.

"I found it," I said in low tones. "It used to house one of the most complete original libraries of medieval manuscripts in Europe. The collection was preserved exactly as it was since 1352." I took a deep, shuddering breath. "That means they would have had your manuscript. Except the library and the whole abbey were destroyed in the Second World War."

The pictures had jarred another memory, of one of many postcards. My parents had been there.

CHAPTER TWELVE

#37: Chalkboard Key Rack
Dimensions: 1.5' x 1.5'
Description: Small chalkboard with hooks for keys
that hung in our foyer. Mom would use it to write
a different message for Dad to see as soon as he
walked in the door.

WE CLIMBED UP all five flights of stairs from the library's most underground level. Each level up had a little more chatter and activity until the top, where students casually conversed in groups. But Bulfinch and I couldn't feel so relaxed.

The light was mellowing into a midafternoon glow that poured in from the library's mostly glass upper story, and the shade between panels of light lengthened and deepened just enough to be cool again. I felt the waves of exhaustion that come after a day in the sun, slightly sad that the afternoon was over and that the happy enchantment of its beginning was gone.

I wondered what Bulfinch must be feeling. There could have been few reminders as stark as this that his time, his home, and everything that was familiar to him was long gone. His life's work had disappeared with barely a trace in a global conflagration hundreds of years after his friends had died. And there was nothing he could do he could do about it. He couldn't prevent it, and he couldn't undo it. Something about the story unsettled me too—something I couldn't quite put my finger on, like a name I couldn't remember.

I wondered if he felt anything like I had when my parents didn't come home; or when the police came to destroy their memory. I wondered if I could share that with him or if it would only seem belittling. My own pain flooded back, after the brief respite that the excitement and novelty of his arrival had given me. It was like waking up, in that moment when the dream is slipping away and you just realized you won't be able to keep it going.

I was jolted out of my thoughts by a blond girl who grabbed my arm as I ascended the steps to the upper-quad exit and she descended on the other side. She seemed familiar, but she chirped hello as if I should know her.

"I'm Allison," she introduced herself cheerfully when she saw I didn't recognize her. "We have Literacy and Notions of Power in the Thirteenth Century together," she prompted. Her face slotted into place then; she was one of the chatty participants in the class near the front of the room. Her kind usually made me sigh and relegate my mind to other things during class. There was no way I could compete with garrulous types like her for attention or a place in the discussion, I thought, so I never tried.

"I never see you outside of class!" she exclaimed. She was as excited as if she'd caught me in the middle of a most delightful bank robbery. "What's the deal? Do you live far away, or are you just new here?"

"Um, no. This is my second semester in the program. I actually live in Hampden. I've been there with my uncle for a little while." I still said "a little while," even though it had been seven years.

"That's funny," Allison replied. "I've never seen you around. I live up in Wyman Park Apartments," she continued. "We could walk to class together!"

"Okay," I said, wondering if the conversation was over. She pulled me in again, though, just when I thought it was safe to leave.

"Who's your friend?" she asked, peering around at Bulfinch. She smiled and waved at him, chirping her introduction again (as if he hadn't been there all along), but he only returned with the weakest of dismal smiles and look a million miles away. I thought that would discourage her, but she seemed oblivious.

"He's kind of an international exchange student," I improvised. "His English isn't very good."

"Where from?" Allison asked.

"Uh, Germany."

"Oh, does he have a really cool German name?"

"You know what, we have to go," I said curtly.

"Well, it was nice meeting you!" she chirped while we bolted up the steps away from her. "I hope I'll see you around! *Auf Weidersehen!*"

It was hyper, social people like her, I thought, that scared me off the whole socializing business in the first place. They were aggressively friendly. I never thought at the time that I defended my shyness just as fiercely.

❧❧

When we got back to the house, I saw Uncle Alvin in the kitchen through the front window. He had come back from Peabody early. He was shoulders deep in the fridge, rooting around.

I cursed under my breath. How was I going to get Bulfinch back upstairs? I veered him toward the side of the house and pushed him into the shadow of the narrow space between our house and the neighbor's, that ended with a rusted-shut gate to the backyard. I waited there with him for a tense five minutes, hoping Uncle Alvin would find what he was looking for and leave the kitchen so we could get in through the front of the house. Then I crept in the front door and had a peek around.

Uncle Alvin had moved to the living room with a jar of olives, reclining to the sound of Grieg's "Piano Concerto in A minor" on the record player. His eyes were gently lidded, and in the shadow cast by the thin curtains, I couldn't tell if he was dozing. I took a deep breath and pattered back out to fetch Bulfinch.

I led Bulfinch back to the door and held my finger to my lips, but he was still despondent and didn't look like he was about to burst into conversation anyway. I pushed the door open and we snuck in, darting on tiptoe down the hall toward the stairs. We were one flight up and I unleashed a sigh of relief, but then I heard Alvin's voice, clear and awake:

"Rosie?"

"Yeah."

"Are you alone?"

"Um, yeah," I called down the stairs, my hand still gripping Bulfinch's hand.

"I thought I heard somebody else."

"Oh. That was just Max," I blurted, cursing myself.

"Who's Max?"

"No one."

I waited until I was sure there would be no more questions, and then a little longer since that was usually about the time Uncle Alvin started asking them again. Then

I clambered the rest of the way up the stairs, attempting a casual tread. Bulfinch didn't question our secretiveness; he was too self-absorbed at the moment to be suspicious. I ushered him into the attic and closed the door behind him. As an afterthought, I locked it for the first time since Bulfinch had returned, not to keep him in, but to keep Alvin out.

I crept back downstairs to get us both glasses of water. The living room reverberated to the finale of the concerto in A minor. Uncle Alvin sat in the middle of a nest of crusade literature. I thought I was safe.

"Humph," he humphed as I walked back toward the stairs. "You've been hiding."

Why did he mention that now? In the seven years we'd lived together, he had gone for weeks sometimes without any sign that he noticed when I was home or away. Then again, for seven years, I had never been away for long. I grumbled under my breath. What was he doing, staking out the hallway from his armchair in the living room? He had never stopped me like this before. Why was he getting inquisitive about my life now? The rage I'd been carrying around in my pocket for him hopped out into my hand again.

"What do you care?" I said without stopping.

"How's class, then?" Uncle Alvin called after me. When he asked about my classes, it meant he was in a bad mood. They were easy targets for his pent sarcasm, especially after silent days in Peabody Library dwelling on its tragedy: it was a beautiful, varied, and historic collection that attracted, at most, only two or three readers a day, a high percentage of whom were addled pseudo-scholars on intellectual grail quests.

I didn't want to have this conversation with him, but the well-trained child in me still couldn't walk away from a question like that. I stopped on the stairs.

"I haven't been," I said. "I mean, I've had a lot of research to do. So I didn't go this week."

"Why bother signing up in the first place?" Alvin barked. "If you're going to go, go. If you're not, then quit."

I'd always known Uncle Alvin didn't have a high opinion of the university, but he had never before told me to drop out. It made me angry. First he's overprotective, then he yells at me for not taking initiative. What the hell was his problem?

"I need to go to school," I said. Alvin didn't respond; he simply cleared his throat phlegmatically and began to read aloud. I let the first few words wash over me before I realized that they were neither Latin nor Greek, Uncle Alvin's usual vocal exercisers. Something familiar about it grabbed a hold of me, and I ran back down the stairs and into the living room.

"What is that?" I asked, the only time I'd ever interrupted his reading since I was a little girl. Uncle Alvin finished a verse before answering, and he kept his eyes fixed on the book while he spoke.

"Die Merseburger Zaubersprüche."

They were in one of my library books upstairs. I saw Uncle Alvin had his own copy. It looked worn—it must have been buried all along in the illogical, uncharted, rambling library that occupied every nook and spare shelf in the house.

"Althochdeutsch," he added, wheezed a little, and took a sip of water. "Old High German, the medieval language of Germany. Two folk magic spells: the first one is for the release of prisoners. The second is to cure a horse's sprain."

I was anxious with the paranoia of a secret-keeper, but also excited.

"They were found on the endpapers of a medieval liturgy. Some bored cleric wrote them there, probably around the ninth century." Uncle Alvin still wasn't looking at me, but he had put the book down and was shuffling through some of those immediately surrounding him, and I knew that this little lecture was compensation for my missed classes. He picked up a volume by Erdmann and turned its pages in silence.

I stood still for a moment, staring at him. Did he stop reading the Old High German on purpose to annoy me, after I'd shown interest in it?

"Don't look so bored, Rosie. Think of what an immense blessing it is to be able to read." He hemmed and turned another page, as if to close his point.

The record faded to an end. We were blanketed in silence. I wanted to do something I knew would irritate him as much as his submersion in his book irritated me. I sat down with a flounce in the armchair next to his and I dug the remote out of the cushions. I turned on the tiny ancient TV tucked in the corner of the room and turned the volume up high. The local news was on.

A female reporter clutching her microphone. Behind her, the scene was totally absurd. Cars covered in grass and bicycle parts were parked in a row while jugglers wandered between neo-Cubist sculptures in a small park near Penn Station.

"This weekend the Mount Vernon landscape has been transformed into an Artscape," the news reporter twittered. "Now in its second decade, the annual Artscape Festival dominates the blocks south of Penn Station in an explosion of color, music, craft, and performance art. And not all of the performances are limited to theater space ..."

The reporter began to walk through the scene, the camera following.

"Here we have roving 'improv impresarios,' comedians, dancers, and plain old eccentrics who take their act into the open air, assuming characters that they use to interact with Artscape visitors. Let's see if we can talk to one."

The reporter turned away from the camera now, revealing the "performer" she had been backing up toward. My jaw dropped. It was Joachim.

"Look at this, a medieval knight in full armor, right here in the middle of Baltimore. Tell us a little about yourself."

She waved the mic in Joachim's face. He growled something in Old German and batted it away, looking suspiciously between the reporter and the camera.

The reporter turned back to the camera with a happy grin on her face.

"It looks like this guy is so far into character that he won't even speak modern English! What an act! He seems to be carrying around a children's history book, and he's showing Artscape patrons a map from 'his time.' I guess we'll have to leave it to the art buffs to interpret this one for us, right, Bob?"

The show cut to a shot of the studio anchor laughing and agreeing with her. He thanked her, and they cut back briefly to Artscape. The reporter was still facing the camera, but Joachim was now prodding her shoulder, which she was trying to cheerfully ignore.

"For WYPA Baltimore, I'm ..." she began.

I didn't hear her finish—nor, for that matter, did the greater Baltimore area—because at that moment, Joachim lost his patience, drew his sword, and swung at the camera.

"I have to go," I told Uncle Alvin, dropping the remote and sprinting upstairs.

CHAPTER THIRTEEN

#127: Sherlock Holmes Hat and Magnifying Glass
Dimensions: glass + handle = 5"
Description: From an old Halloween costume my mom
  wore.

WE NEEDED TO MOVE FAST. It was obvious that Joachim's behavior would not continue without repercussions, and I had to make sure I made it to him before anyone else did. But I couldn't bring him back by myself. I'd have no way of explaining to him why he needed to follow me. I'd need Bulfinch as an interpreter—and as back-up.

Alvin was still in the living room, within sight of the garden through the back windows of the house, so climbing out the fire escape and down that way was out of the question. The best thing to try, I decided, was to make a solid break for it the way we had entered the house, which we did, after creeping gently down the stairs. Once outside, we dashed to the nearest bus stop and caught the first bus to Mount Vernon. When we were seated, I finally found the time and breath to tell Bulfinch what our mission was.

The news was distressing for us both, but the urgency lifted the bleakness from Bulfinch's face. For a little bit, he could lose himself in the adventure, and forget what he had learned this afternoon.

I hadn't stayed long enough to see the reactions of the studio anchors or staff to the knight's outburst; I didn't even know if the camera was his only victim. I could only hope that his anger had spent itself on the hunk of plastic; and that, when it became clear that he would be apprehended, he lost himself in the crowd. Once out of sight of the witnesses, he might have some chance of blending in. Artscape wasn't the only place he could have stumbled into where his get-up would have fit in. For the third time in three years, Otakon, one of America's biggest anime conventions, was held in the Baltimore Convention Center on the same weekend as Artscape, and many of its patrons were emerging from the center to hunt up dinner among the cultural district's trendy restaurants. The streets were flooded with people in strange costumes, with a liberal distribution of swords and armor.

I imagined Joachim rampaging through the festival like John Cleese's hyper-violent Lancelot through the peaceful wedding in *Monty Python and the Holy Grail*.

When we arrived, Bulfinch pulled his hat down low over his face, as if he were the one hiding. I thought I understood why; previously, the sight of him had sent the knight running, and now more than ever it was imperative that we catch him and bring him safely home.

A few blocks south of the train station, we found the predictable clot of police officers taking statements from witnesses. It was hard to see into the crowd as we skirted it, trying to avoid attention, but I couldn't help myself—I jumped on a bench and peered over the heads to see if everyone was intact. It looked like the reporter and her cameraman, though seriously shaken, were unharmed. I breathed a sigh of relief.

I also hadn't seen Joachim in the cluster, which made me hope that he had gotten away. No one in the area seemed to be chasing or looking for him; maybe he had made a clean getaway. Where he could be hiding, however, was beyond me. I was reluctant to ask if anyone had seen him because I didn't want anyone else on his trail.

We walked straight down Charles Street, our eyes peeled for the smallest clue. I'm not sure what we expected to find; a shred of his tunic on a thorn bush?

We weren't alone in our search. Police officers were crawling all over the festival, asking bewildered arts patrons and samurai if they'd seen a medieval knight.

I picked up the pace, and we slipped ahead of the closest officer near the far end of the festival, where the food vendors were all parked together in a lot surrounding picnic tables. It was then that I saw a flash of metallic light, like the one that had caught my eye years ago in the woods by Beauview Drive. A moment later, my eyes adjusted to the brightness of the unshaded lot, and I saw him at the very end arguing (probably unsatisfactorily) with a sausage vendor.

Bulfinch saw him too. But I also caught, out of the corner of my eye, a police officer chatting with a vendor to our left. He was facing away, and from his angle, he probably couldn't see the knight because of the various tents between; fortunately, the vendor he was speaking to had missed Joachim too.

I grabbed Bulfinch's arm just as he was about to launch himself toward the knight at the opposite end of the lot. He followed my lead and we power-walked across the food court, a bit faster than casual but not as attention-grabbing as a full run. As we neared, we heard Joachim and his opponent's voices rise to shouts.

Just as Joachim was about to reach over the stall, Bulfinch shouted something to him that made him freeze. I froze too, wondering what Bulfinch's plan was, fearing that it would draw more stares. Bulfinch continued his speech in Old German, and the knight turned to him, an unexpected look of fear on his face. Bulfinch lifted his cap, and Joachim nearly dropped to his knees. Bulfinch rushed forward and dragged him into a nearby alley while I scampered behind, just as the police officers began approaching Joachim's sausage antagonist.

We ran a few blocks east until I felt safe. Then we paused in a narrow alley. Surprisingly again, Joachim idled there with us passively, darting glances at Bulfinch.

I caught my breath. Then I asked, "What did you tell him?"

"Nothing but some pagan superstition to convince him to join us."

I thought for a second and put the scene together in my mind.

"Wait. He ran that first night because he *recognized you*. And then when you talked to him today, he came with us because he *recognized you*. You two know each other."

"Impossible!" Bulfinch exclaimed unconvincingly.

"Exactly. You told me he came from a story a novice told you years ago. About a knight who was there years before that."

"It's possible there was some slight exaggeration involved," Bulfinch mumbled.

"I need you to tell me the truth. All of it. If I'm going to help either of you get home, not to mention keep him out of scrapes like this, I need to know everything," I said.

"Well, if you narrate events exactly as they occurred, then I would be the novice. And it's also possible that I was personally offended by a particular knight's barbarity at table and at prayer. And that when that knight left this novice's abbey, the novice, who could also be referred to as myself, told that knight that he would be cursed for his unpleasantness by our holy patron."

I paused to digest it all. "Why didn't you tell me all this earlier?" I asked.

"My other version is better," he said. "More elegant and foreboding." His veneer melted away under my hard look. "And that one wasn't completely my fault."

"What *did* you tell him just now?" I asked one more time.

"Hrm," he squeaked. "That first night when he ran from me, I deduced that it was because he feared me, believing that I had personally inflicted this curse upon him. A few minutes ago, I may have led him to believe that I could do so again with even more terrible consequences if he didn't cooperate. I believe we've reached a satisfying arrangement now."

I slumped against the wall. The sun was sinking and the street lights were turning on. I had a vague feeling that Bulfinch's tactic was unethical, but I couldn't bring myself to care.

"Let's go home," I groaned, and led the way.

On our way back, just to round off the day, I ran into Allison again. She was heading home to her apartment a few blocks from my house, and she couldn't contain her ebullience at seeing me and my friend again. I knew better than to linger this time, though, and I trudged ahead, pretending not to hear her cheerfully shouted questions about my second friend and his funny clothes. At least she hadn't been near a TV in the last hour, I hoped.

❧❦

Uncle Alvin had abandoned the living room by the time we returned. It was easy to glide in the back door and up to the attic unseen. Once there, I began immediately stripping the knight of his squeaky (and now, identifying) armor. Joachim didn't protest. Instead, he just shot sidelong, nervous glances at Bulfinch.

I left them together while I fetched food and extra bedding. I hoped I would return to find them both in one piece. To my relief and wonder, when I popped back into the attic, they were sitting on opposite sides of the room, Bulfinch happily reading, Joachim slightly despondently looking out the window. Snap a picture, I thought, and you have a pre-Raphaelite tableau.

As I set down the dinner things and beckoned the now-subdued Joachim to the table, I thought of another question to ask Bulfinch.

"If you both disappeared at the same time, presumably," I said, "Why did you think that asking him 'the end' of his story would fix everything? He probably doesn't know the end any better than you do."

Bulfinch sighed.

"I chased him because he was the only thing I recognized when I found myself in this bizarre place," he said. "And I encouraged you to recapture him because you seemed the kindest and friendliest person here, the one most capable of helping us."

"So you never thought that finding him would—reverse whatever spell brought you here?" I prompted.

"I only thought that it would be most fair if the two of us suffered our strange fate together," he said. "And without another person from my time, I would feel—very lost."

Sympathy for him washed away whatever irritation was left about his "exaggerations."

"So, we're back to square one," I said, looking at the knight packing away food. Bulfinch nodded.

"How many squares are there?" he asked.

CHAPTER FOURTEEN

#56: Pet Rock
Dimensions: 1" x 2"
Description: "Create your own friend!"

I SLUMPED DOWN to my bedroom, drained of ideas. And guiltily relieved. When we had been chasing Joachim, as stressful as it was, it was a real adventure. And I had the cooperation of a real sidekick, a medieval visitor who, unlike Joachim, wanted to communicate with me. The excitement and the novelty had made me lose sight of our original goal: to find a way to return Bulfinch and Joachim to their own time.

It was already dim in my curtained room. I flipped on the light and yelped—Max was sitting on my bed, examining a teddy bear.

"What are you doing here?" I whispered, my heart still hammering from the shock.

"I showed up for our promenade after a slight delay, but you'd gone walksies on me. I got bored later and came back, but you were out. So I climbed in the back window and waited for you."

"You climbed in? And came up to my room?"

"Yeah. I didn't want to run into your uncle."

I sat down and took the teddy bear out of her hands, throwing it to the other side of the bed.

"Why are you here? Why did you break into my house and wait for me?" I asked again, starting to feel angry.

"It's not your house," Max replied. "It's your uncle's. Anyway, I was in the neighborhood and I was hot, so I came in and got myself a glass of water. Show a little hospitality. I just wanted to come out of the sun."

We sat tensely in silence, but it didn't last long; Max never showed up for silent companionship. She existed to talk, to draw me out and ask questions and make me explain myself.

"How was your grand tour?" she asked, picking up another stuffed animal, a bunny this time, and tweaking its ears to see how firmly they were attached.

"It was pleasant," I began, but I didn't really want to talk about it with her. The impressions were so sweet—until our discovery in the library—that I didn't want to share with Max. Talking to Max slanted everything. "What kept you?" I asked, changing the subject.

"Class," Max mumbled, now testing the strength of the bunny's other facial features. One beady black eye came out in her fingers and became a button.

My ears sang and I had a sickening, sinking feeling, like I was tobogganing down a slick slope to a cliff. Class. I hadn't been to any classes in days. But Max jogged my memory; graduate students in my department were supposed to be seeking teaching assistant positions this term, and I couldn't remember the deadline. I dove under my bed, where most of my syllabi and other school materials lived, and hunted for the paperwork, determined to fill it out that night. Max seemed amused. I glared at her.

"What were *you* doing in class?" I asked her. "You never go to class."

"*Au contraire, mon ami*," she said. "I only go to class when you don't. That's why you never see me there."

I opened up my laptop before I remembered its accident earlier that week. Foolishly hoping that rest had cured it, I pounded the power key a few times. It made a sad whirring noise again, its indicator lights flashed, and then it died. I realized I hadn't checked my email in all the trips I'd made to the library since the other day; I'd been too absorbed in research.

I also realized with a sinking feeling that the only copy of the first chapter of my thesis on the multi-perspective approach to ethics and philosophy in Peter Abelard's Sic et Non had been saved on that computer. My latest draft had been due three days ago. I hadn't written a word to my advisor.

I was drawing short breaths now, and I felt the color drain from my face. I remembered Uncle Alvin's rebuke and wondered if I really should drop out—if I simply didn't have the discipline and focus to belong in a school, to waste my time and resources and money, and Uncle Alvin's too, on something I neglected like a big expensive toy.

Worse still, I thought of my mother—she had given up her Ph.D. and dropped out of graduate school to marry my dad. Did she feel this way when it happened? Or was it all right, because she was moving on to something new and different in life, rather than hiding everything.

She did, she did, a voice whispered in my mind. *She hid too. She hid more than you know. She left school to steal money from other people. She ran away. She ran away from the blame, and she ran away from you.* My stomach felt sick. I tried to silence the voice, but it was like swatting at a fly that always zipped to the other side of the room when you thought you had it.

Max nosed the bunny against my cheek. At first I turned away, but soon enough she raised a weak smile, and I snatched the bunny away, stroking its soft ears through my fingers while I looked down at it on my lap.

"Don't get angsty on me," she chirped, turning toward me on the bed and folding her legs. "You're a good kid."

"Yeah," I mumbled.

"You haven't done anything really bad. It's not like you crashed a car or got into drugs."

"Mmm-hmm," I murmured, taking a deep breath.

"And you've got a good excuse, even if you can't tell it to your advisor. I mean, the whole point of school is learning, and you've been studying history in the flesh," Max continued, her voice becoming more strident.

"Yeah," I said, putting the bunny down. "I've been working really hard."

"And you have a lot of responsibility. You're taking care of a whole person."

"Yeah. I know! Two of them!"

"All that teaching stuff and essay stuff is just paperwork. So what if your draft is late or you need to fill out some dumb application form? That doesn't mean you're stupid!"

"I don't have time for that crap!" I exclaimed, feeling much better. "I'm smarter than that!"

Max bounced once on the bed, and I felt a little better, squeezing my bunny doll.

"Okay, let's get down to our real business," she said. "Get the Letter, let's figure out where Bulfinch is from."

"We have a mission," I called happily as I bounded out of my room and down the stairs to fetch the bag containing my letter notebook.

I came back bearing my treasure, in better spirits. In fact, I felt a thrill down my back and a bubbling sensation from my knees upward that converged to wash away the sickening guilt I'd felt moments earlier. Our mission—Max's and mine—was to find the truth If classes conflicted with that, they were just a distraction from something grander.

Max's manic fascination was contagious. I tore the envelope out of the notebook with a new energy—I usually treated it respectfully, delicately, like an ancient manuscript. I rustled the folded paper out of the envelope and dropped it open, and what I saw made me turn cold, instantly, like a shower of ice.

The page that had been covered, on both sides, with Bulfinch's story, was now blank.

"Oh dear," Max said dryly as we looked at it. "That's going to make things a bit harder."

It was the only clue I had had to discovering where my visitors had come from and how to get them back, but it stared back up at me, clean like a parchment sanded down as a palimpsest, waiting to be rewritten.

"I should have known," I couldn't stop myself from saying aloud. I set the blank page on my comforter with shaking hands, as I had seven years ago when I'd first read it. I drew an uncertain breath. "At least now we know for sure that the page is how he got here."

After all, why else would it have cleared itself? Its contents were out of its prison and walking around now.

Max flopped backward onto the bed.

"I knew all along," she said. "They got here through your head because you knew that story so well it became part of your brain—you don't need the Letter anymore to remember the story. You believed it so thoroughly that it became real."

What Max said had once been true, but I realized with deepening panic that it was almost as if the knight's appearance had taken the story out of me, just like it had erased it from the page. The law of the conservation of matter applied here, and this imaginative matter could not exist in two places at the same time—I would either have the story in my head, or the knight in my attic, but not both at the same time. I was left with a composition book full of physical descriptions of the Letter, but I had never copied out its actual words.

"But I can't ask him his own story," I said. "He doesn't know how it ends yet."

"You can remember what happened when he appeared," Max replied. "You can remember what you saw."

I did, vividly on the edge of my mental vision, like a bright thing caught out of the corner of my eye. When I turned toward it, it fled once more to the periphery, but it was there, certainly, the memory of that hallucination, a monster of other memories grown over each other.

"Try it again," Max whispered. "Make another one."

I wanted to roll my eyes, but instead I closed them. I realized I had to know if it had been my imagination that had summoned those two and if I could do it again. If it was possible to summon Bulfinch and Joachim, maybe it was possible to summon my parents as I had known them—and to clear their names. I tried to reconstruct the images I saw in my mind when the knight and the monk appeared.

Imagine a birchwood, I told myself. Summer sunlight slants through translucent leaves. The air is green and peaceful.

A knight stands between the trees straight and tall. His helmet glints dully. He looks toward nothing with gray eyes. His face is grave, his mouth a hard line but not cruel. His tunic rises and falls rhythmically, minutely. His heart beats silently.

Ferns wash around his calves. The smell of crushed ferns rises from the ground and curls into his nostrils. The woods are still. The knight is still. The ferns tremble. The knight breathes.

I opened my eyes slowly, trembling with anticipation. But no one had appeared. I noted that the light had grown dimmer and the air cooler in the meantime, and I stretched my legs and pointed my toes, surprised by how stiff and dead they felt. Had I fallen asleep?

I had to know the truth. I had to find some other document that proved to me that Joachim and his chronicler had existed after this episode in their lives. I had to piece together what it meant and how they got here, so I could send them home—and bring my parents home too. I needed to find the rest of the book that I had been searching for from the age of twelve.

I gasped when I turned onto my side and felt a slip of paper crinkle underneath me.

I picked it up. On it was a phone number and Uncle Alvin's terse message: "Detective Harrison call ASAP"

CHAPTER FIFTEEN

#16: Hourglass
Dimensions: 3" tall
Description: Lost from some game; origin unknown.

HE SAID IT would be better to discuss the findings in person. That's the way doctors deliver the worst news, I thought. He suggested coming back to the house, returning whatever of my parents' papers the investigators could spare and then staying to sit and talk it over in the kitchen, where I'd be comfortable. I didn't want any of them coming back here.

Oddly, my biggest fear in leaving the house was not what the detective would tell me in the diner I had chosen, but how Joachim and Bulfinch would fare in the hours without me. Coolly, logically, I knew that they both understood it was in their best interests to remain, quiet, in the attic and that the knight had reached an impasse in his distrust of the monk. But at the same time I was convinced that when I returned they would be gone with the same suddenness with which they had appeared. That without my attention, they would vanish. I used this worry to smother the anguish in my mind that kept trying to get free and grip me, a monster with my parents' faces.

I went. I went because the next morning I saw Uncle Alvin, and when he looked at me across the space between his seat on the patio and where I stood on the other side of the open door, near the stairs, I saw he knew about the neglected emails from my professors, the skipped classes, the plunging grades, the broken appointments, as side effects of my absence from his lessons, and his eyes asked, "Are you skipping this too?" I was resentful as if he had physically shoved me out the door, but I went.

The yellow flicker of cheap fluorescent lights in the diner made my head pound. The table was white Formica, and the mugs were plain white with one blue stripe. I think I had wanted it to look like a film noir so I could fictionalize this episode too, shelve it until I chose how and when to incorporate it into my parents' lives. Anyway, if we were someplace public, I might be able to resist the urge to scream or cry.

I swallowed each word Detective Harrison served to me and slowly allowed it to begin to digest, to mingle with the matter of my existing beliefs. All I allowed myself was a nod, a hum of understanding, while the case was laid before me.

My dad had been funneling money out of his office for years, years before I had even been born, and he had kept it in cash, trickling it out in extravagant gifts rather than traceable financial investments. There were no signs that my mother had been explicitly aware of the fraud, but her ignorance of it was suspicious.

I remembered sitting at the kitchen table and looking at my parents and feeling so happy that they were so in love with each other. I remember that feeling wrapped around me like a huge, soft quilt. Now all the times I'd seen his eyes shine as she opened a little box and her smile spread in warmth and gratitude were a betrayal. I was never a part of those moments. They were part of a secret my parents kept from me.

The truth hadn't just darkened those individual moments. It spread through the memory of my childhood like a poison until I questioned whether my parents had ever loved me at all. My ears started ringing. My face and my hands went numb. The wall-builders inside my mind were paralyzed too. There was nothing I could do to protect myself from now.

Detective Harrison told me the police would reopen the investigation into my parents' disappearance. It was a formality, the detective assured me, to soften what came next. They simply had to confirm there were no obvious signs that they had meant to vanish with the money.

I used to wish my parents were alive somewhere, waiting to be found. Now I hoped they were dead.

&c&s&

When I was twelve, I asked my mom where history came from. Earlier that summer, inspired by NOVA, I'd asked where orange juice, cars, faxes, and houses came from, as if these were all commodities that grew in the ground, were pulled up and shipped to consumers.

"I'm impressed, young lady," she said. "Mostly people never think to ask that question at all."

We were stretched out in the sun on the yard again.

"Well," my mom continued, "First the historian looks at what others have written about the period, to familiarize himself with what's already been discovered or surmised."

"What if it's wrong?"

"We'll get to that. Because next he looks at documents from the era he's studying—journals, letters, maps, chronicles, proclamations, and the histories written by the people who saw it first hand."

"What if they're lying too?" I asked the questions lying on my back, looking at the trees between my fingers. I asked idly, and my mom answered eagerly.

"Well, that's a good question. Sometimes they manipulate the truth to flatter their rulers or minimize their losses. Sometimes what sounds like an exaggeration is just a factor of their lack of knowledge. For example, a ruler's historian might write that the whole world was gathered under his wings, but at that time, the whole world (or what was worth mentioning of it) might have been the lands immediately bordering the Mediterranean."

A robin flew to its nest halfway up our tree. I watched it with its young. I asked my mom another question.

"So, how do you know?"

"Well, part of it is deduction. You can assume, by the whole world, he can't mean parts of the world yet undiscovered by Europeans. And then there's archaeological evidence. Like solving a crime. There are things left behind. You can tell how far an empire expanded by how far its coins were distributed, or where its soldiers were encamped, or where people build their houses and forts. You can find out a lot from burial grounds, trash heaps, abandoned camps, old roads, and ancient churches. It's like a puzzle of information, and the historian learns to put it all together."

My eyelids were growing heavy, but I never wanted to fall asleep, ever, when there were so many things I could be feeding into my mind and senses awake.

"What if all the pieces don't fit together? What if some of them are missing?"

My mom paused for the first time in our conversation, without a ready answer. I could hear the distant rumble of traffic on the highway miles away.

"Then the historian should have the courage to admit he doesn't know something," she said at last, but I wasn't sure if it was part of a dream.

✧✧✧

The cold bright florescent light of the diner seemed to be buzzing, louder and louder, or maybe it was just the singing in my ears. I would not look Detective Harrison in the face. I glared at my coffee mug.

"Is there enough evidence to convict them if you do find them?" I asked. "Or is this all just some sort of hunch you want to prove by digging them up somewhere?"

Tears were running down my face. It was as if my eyes were leaking and I couldn't stop them. If I didn't focus my mind on any one thing, I wouldn't break into sobs, my face wouldn't convulse; I knew if those things happened I'd be uncontrollable. Instead, the tears just flowed and flowed. I was perplexed, outside myself. I was standing outside myself looking at my pain and wondering, *Why won't my eyes stop streaming? When will they run out of water?*

"All the evidence for the fraud is in the papers we found in your attic," Detective Harrison replied. "However, if you want my personal hunch, your parents didn't run away. The fact that they left everything behind intact and made no attempt to destroy or hide it further says to me they weren't looking to disappear just yet. But we have to look into it."

"You did look into it," I said, my voice shaking, surprising myself. The harder I tried to steady it, the more it wavered and broke. "Didn't you look hard enough before? Is there something you didn't try back then? They told me they must be dead by now." My face convulsed. I couldn't stop myself anymore. "I already let them die," I sobbed. "I let them die in my mind. They're gone. They're dead to me. Just leave them alone."

❧❦

My parents had been legally declared dead right before I started my first semester of graduate study, the previous fall.

At Loyola, I was used to my professors treating me with a distanced awe. A more cheerful or outgoing student, even by a little bit, would have made them much more comfortable. But I was cold toward them, to the point of hostility, after years of Alvin's carefully sown disdain for institutional learning. After my freshman year, no one asked about my personal life.

Hopkins was different. Nobody knew me, so I had to start over establishing the buffer of aloofness that protected me from personal questions. My age didn't help in deflecting attention.

"You're my first nineteen-year-old master's scholar," Professor Thomas Charlemagne said to me with a sincere smile in our first meeting to discuss my course of study.

"Ph.D. candidate," I corrected. "It's a Master's-Ph.D. program."

Professor Charlemagne raised his eyebrows, but his smile didn't waver.

"Let's take one step at a time," he said. "See where the studies take us."

I didn't respond.

"Now, I don't like to pry," he continued, seemingly unflappable, "But I do think it helps if we get to know each other a little bit first—so you can tell me what your goals are, what you hope to accomplish, what drew you to history. I'm not just grading your papers; this is a relationship. Over the next few years, I can help you take this bud of interest and inspiration and let it blossom into a career and serious accomplishments."

I didn't respond.

"So," he said, leaning back with a faint falter in his eyes at last, "Tell me your story. I'd love to know how a nineteen-year-old came to this position. Are your parents historians?"

"My mom studied history."

Professor Charlemagne recovered the gleam in his smile.

"I bet she must be very proud of you," he said.

"My parents were just legally declared dead," I said, in a deadpan tone that I hoped would discourage further questioning. "A month ago."

Professor Charlemagne stared blankly for a few moments. His smile disappeared completely.

"I'm so sorry for your loss," he said with warmth, his eyebrows furrowing as he leaned forward.

"They've been gone for a long time," I replied.

"You know," he said quietly, "You can get free counseling in the health center. It's available to all students. Have you spoken to someone?"

I blinked. It took me a moment to process what he meant. I wasn't used to euphemisms like "counseling" or "talk to someone."

"You mean therapy?" I asked, a bit angrily. "You're asking if I've had therapy?"

"I just wanted to make sure you're aware it's available," he said. "Lots of students use it. Professors too. You don't have to tell me if you do or not. I won't ask again. I just remember when my ..." His voice faltered. "When my mother passed away, well, I had my sister and my dad to talk to and my friends to support me, but some things are so private, so hurting, you ... you want to talk to someone impartial, someone professional who won't judge you, who can help you understand what you're going through and teach you how to deal with your new life."

I stared at him. "My new life?" I'd been stuck with Alvin for seven years. "Professional?" Who's a professional on feelings? What is there to understand? Feelings come into you, you experience them, then they float away sometimes if you're lucky. It all seemed obvious to me. My parents had been gone for seven years. I had missed them every day. My life was gray and friendless. I felt like I was sinking through the ground all the time. What would thirty minutes with a stranger and a box of tissues teach me about that?

Professor Charlemagne quickly changed the subject back to my course of study, which we discussed for an hour without straying from the topic again. He was true to his word: he never again asked me if I'd visited the counselor.

That first night, though, when I'd walked home, the professor's words lingered in my mind, especially "I had my sister and my dad and my friends to support me." What did I have to support me? Would it hurt so much to talk to Alvin about it? I was a little afraid of him. He'd shown no emotion the day he filled out the paperwork, and I thought that meant he'd disapprove if I showed any emotion, either. I thought the appropriate way to respond to this change was to pretend nothing had happened. In the physical sense, nothing had changed. It was embarrassing to care so much about his signature on a few sheets of paper, doing nothing more than assert what we already knew: they had been gone for seven years.

Then why did it feel like something had gone rotten inside me and it was poisoning my blood? Why did I stop looking both ways when I crossed the street, stop caring if

I could be mugged if I walked through the park at night? Why hadn't I showered in three days? Why hadn't I eaten in two? Every morning I woke up with bruised-feeling eyes, brimming but not spilling over, wishing, begging my body to let me cry. But I didn't.

I opened the front door, letting in the fresh, sweet, leaf rot smelling autumn breeze. The house was full of dim blue twilight. I heard Alvin listening to records in the living room in the back. As I stepped through the door, I rehearsed in my mind what I would say. "Are you sad too? Or am I the only one?"

I crept toward the living room. Every creak of the floor sent a jolt to my heart. Lately, every little noise, however ordinary, scared me like a gunshot.

In the living room, only one dim orange light was on. Alvin sat just outside its pool of light. His eyes were closed, his big eyebrows pulled together. He was conducting to the record. His head nodded and tilted slightly to the mournful strains of music. His hands didn't fly through the air dramatically, but they stayed close to the arms of the chair, his big green armchair, the mate of which had been his wife's seat. His hands waved gently, minutely, an extension of the aching melody.

"Uncle Alvin," I said quietly, but loud enough to be heard over the music. "Uncle Alvin," I tried again. He didn't open his eyes. I left him there, more despondent then I'd ever been in my life.

The next week, I made an appointment with the counselor as an experiment. No matter how foolish it made me feel, I thought I couldn't possibly feel worse than I did already. The first meeting was just a preliminary—they wouldn't use the word 'assessment,' with its judgmental overtones, but that's what it was. Thirty minutes with a young female counselor not much older than some of the students she probably had to treat. I told her briefly, dryly, the story of my parents' disappearance, how I moved in with Alvin, and how he'd recently declared my parents dead. The therapist asked me a few questions, then suggested we hold a memorial service for my parents. She said it would give us closure to the incident and allow us to move on. I imagined what Alvin would say if I suggested a memorial service, how he'd think it was a farce when we never really knew what had happened to parents and it'd been seven whole years for me to get used to the idea. I never mentioned it to him, and I never went back to the counselor.

I was sobbing uncontrollably in a diner with a detective across the booth from me.

I could barely breathe. Air came in angry gulps. The crying took a hold of me and fed itself. It was like something inside me had been torn open, massively, and raw pain flooded out from an infinite source. I couldn't talk and I could barely hear. I assume Detective Harrison paid the bill because in a few minutes, his hand at my elbow helped me slide out of the booth, and he escorted me to his car. I didn't object. I barely saw what was going on around me. I assume the other customers must have stared.

Detective Harrison drove me home. By the time he pulled up, the sobs had died down, but my face was still twisted and blotched and my throat too tight to talk. He opened the car door for me and walked me to the front step. He pressed a business card into my hand.

"Call me if you have any more questions," he said. "Take some time to process everything, and we can talk more if there's anything you want to know."

I held the card without looking at it and opened the door to the house. Inside it was dark except for one light in the kitchen. I didn't hear the car pull away; I never turned around to say goodbye.

CHAPTER SIXTEEN

#234: Flashlight
Dimensions: 7" long, 0.75" diameter
Description: For reading books under the covers after
  "lights out"

WHEN I CAME in the door, Uncle Alvin was waiting for me in the kitchen with a steaming mug of tea that I suspected he hadn't made for himself. I didn't stop for him. I didn't care how he felt about it or his weak attempts to comfort me after too long of ignoring my pain. I felt possessive of this tragedy as if it were mine alone.

On the second floor, I turned toward my room, but when I put my hand on the doorknob, I was flooded with dread. I couldn't bear to be alone. I thought if I were alone right now, I would die.

Instead, I bolted once more for the attic. Bulfinch and Joachim were real and solid; I could depend on them more than the ghosts of my parents.

Bulfinch and Joachim were working on a jigsaw puzzle I had left out for them. It was a picture of a castle in Scotland that Uncle Alvin had once visited. I stood in the door and looked at them for a long time; they were so used to me coming and going that they only glanced up briefly, and in the dim light they couldn't have seen my face well. I walked to my little burrow of cushions and blankets in the corner and curled into a ball. My eyes drifted open and closed; when they closed for too long, I became afraid, and I forced them open so I could look at my friends and be comforted again. Eventually I dropped into a dreamless sleep.

I woke up sometime in the middle of the night. Joachim was snoring softly in the armchair. Bulfinch was still up, bending over the puzzle. I had no idea what time it was, except that it was late.

I crept up to the table and sat on the floor beside Bulfinch, so my head was almost resting on his knee. I could tell now from the look in his eyes that he'd seen my face when I'd walked in, but he'd given me space. Now he looked down at me with concern, but I didn't want to explain what had happened, so I started discussing what we knew about the magic or miracle that had brought him here.

"It can't just be me," I said. "Otherwise I would have been popping out imaginary figures all over the place. It must have been the book, and something about that moment that made it more ... real. Real enough to leap off the page."

"Are you suggesting," Bulfinch said nervously, "That we weren't real in your world, in your history, before?"

"Of course not," I responded. "I just meant something that pulled you out of your time and into mine."

But I did have some doubts. I was certain that Bulfinch and Joachim were real *now*, but before? I didn't even know if the letter had come from a real history book, or if it was the product of an elaborate hoax. There was nothing left of St. Vitus' Abbey to prove my friend had existed. His history may seem real to him, but it could just have been fiction in my world, my version of reality. I wasn't about to rule out any possibilities. And Bulfinch didn't have a sterling record of telling the truth, especially about himself.

Bulfinch stood up and paced up and down the attic, head down.

"There must be some way of learning what becomes of us," he said. "If we return to our time, then our tales are already over, and I am certain I never would have stopped writing about a life as exciting as mine has clearly already become. Something, somewhere, a remainder of the tale must tell us how we returned. Where is the rest of this book from which you received a page?"

"I've looked for it for years," I groaned. "It doesn't exist."

Bulfinch stopped suddenly.

"Does it truly not exist," he said, "Or do you say that to make it more exciting?"

Great thoughts coming from a class-A fibber, I thought. But I couldn't help realizing he had a point.

"I've tried everything," I said. "I searched the internet, libraries, the bibliographies of other books ... nothing."

"What about this great university you're attached to," Bulfinch prompted. "Have you asked help from any of the scholars there?"

"No," I mumbled. I had always savored the thrill of going solo on my search. It also saved me the embarrassment of explaining everything in the first place.

"Well, ask your mentors there. And what do you know about the intended recipient of this letter?"

"Nothing. The address doesn't exist. No one by that name lives anywhere that even sounds similar, and at any rate they didn't know anyone named Vita and none of them claimed the letter." I bit my tongue before I added on that I didn't think Joe Creekman existed, either. I prickled at little at Bulfinch's casual evaluation of my years of investigation. But I was alo beginning to see his point— how I had intentionally avoided certain approaches not because I had good reason, but because I was afraid of what I would find out, that maybe it would end the chase.

"Perhaps the address is a—what was the phrase you taught me? —red herring," he said. "Irrelevant to the case. Focus on the name. You tried to pinpoint locals who may have been the intended recipient of the letter, but you didn't try to identify the addressee himself. Perhaps he is a scholar who would have been interested in the oddity. Perhaps he is even someone attached to your family, and his correspondent meant all along for the Letter to be sent to you and achieved that despite its misdirection."

"We don't know any Joe Creekmans," I muttered. "My mom would have jumped on that immediately."

"Perhaps it was someone your mother didn't know," Bulfinch pressed. "Your father, or..."

"Why do you have all the smart ideas?" I snapped. But just as quickly I softened. "You love to write fiction," I said gently when I saw Bulfinch's enthusiasm drain away pitifully at my rebuke. "In the space of time you've been here, you've spun me enough tales to make my head spin. Why are you so methodical about these facts?"

Bulfinch sighed, as if uncertain himself.

"Because I'm so good a making things up, I suppose I can consider every possibility. Only one of my suggestions can be true, we just have to find out which one."

We heard a crash. On the other side of the room, Joachim had knocked his puzzle off the tabletop and, when he saw our stares, growled at us. He seemed to be a fan of the "obstacle, meet floor" method of problem-solving.

Something still seemed to bother Bulfinch from our conversation.

"I want you to know," he said, "That for every story I spin, weave, and embellish, I have the truth in my heart. Sometimes it weighs on me terribly."

❧

The next morning, Uncle Alvin was gone again before I woke up. He left the same note on the kitchen table, about going to the Peabody Library. This time a crumb of stale toast and a few grease stains on the paper marked his passage.

I left Bulfinch and Joachim with free range over the attic and the third floor, confident that Uncle Alvin wouldn't be back until late. Bulfinch was captivated by the Museum, and I longed to take him to a real museum, like the Walters or the little historic house on campus, except I was still troubled by the logistical difficulty of getting him in and out of Alvin's house unnoticed. Joachim couldn't come with us if we went anyway in case someone recognized him. Only a few days in this century and he was already a reality TV star.

That day I was leaving my guests to drop in on my faculty advisor's office hours.

I hadn't even written to him to explain the absence of my Peter Abelard paper. It was a project I had only vaguely outlined to him at the beginning of the year, and I had tried to fly under the radar ever since to retain the freedom to research whatever I wanted. He was unused to students so totally refusing faculty support, but at the time I dismissed his doubts. I knew I was different, that I would get it done. Then I didn't.

I walked to his office with a sense of impending doom. I hoped we could get past the awkward discussion of my academic standing quickly enough so I could lose myself in the renewed investigation of Joe Creekman.

"Why, hello there," Professor Charlemagne greeted me cheerfully. I felt comforted by the fact that he didn't seem upset to see me. Thomas Charlemagne was a young faculty member, in his mid-thirties, but to my relief he seemed to avoid the pop-cultural pandering that many of the older staff resorted to in order to hold the attention of their students. Charlemagne, on the other hand, was a little meek, but more than a little kind, with a genuine passion for history. He would have made a great advisor if I'd needed one, I thought. But I had never felt the urge to compete for a professor's attention like my peers.

Charlemagne had stood at my knock, an old-fashioned gesture, and now he sat down again, a curious smile on his face. Behind him, I saw a poster for History: Illuminated, his undergraduate seminar on medieval philosophy. Unlike other professors, he didn't plaster his office with promotional materials for his own books. Now that I thought about it, I couldn't even remember his personal area of study. I vaguely recalled he was famous for discovering some unread and unloved medieval poet.

"So, what brings you here today?" he asked. "It's quite an honor that you made an appearance."

"Yeah, I'm sorry. I've been busy with family ... stuff." I felt a stab of guilt for nearly using the mother of all unquestionable excuses: family emergency. That wouldn't have been crying wolf. It would have been like printing and distributing a Worldwide Fictional Wolf Alert Newsletter. It was a depth of chicanery I was unwilling to plumb.

"I just sent you an email," he continued brightly. He was also one of the few professors who understood the importance of prompt correspondence. "I was expecting to see your Abelard dissection in my inbox this week. What happened?"

"My computer broke," I said, not untruthfully. I didn't have to tell him a medieval knight broke it.

"Oh dear," he groaned. "Did you have a backup of the paper?"

"No," I replied. "But I still have all my materials, and I kept my notes in a marble pad so I haven't lost my research," I piled on breathlessly. *Just push through this part*, I told myself. *Get it out of the way and then we can talk about important things, not irrelevant details like deadlines and grades.* "I can crank out another draft in two weeks."

Charlemagne's face settled into a thoughtful frown.

"I don't like this," he said. "I'm sorry, but I've already extended your deadline twice."

"I couldn't help it," I whined. "My computer broke!"

Charlemagne leaned forward.

"Now, listen to me for a moment. I don't want you to feel like you're being personally persecuted. It's far from pleasant for me to mark down a promising student like yourself—more unpleasant than you can probably guess. But I can't treat you differently from my other students just because you show intellectual promise. You also have to display discipline and academic rigor, motivation and hard work. I can't let you get away with this behavior while my other advisees are working night and day to complete their papers on time."

"Just give me one week..."

"No. I'm sorry. It can't be done. Unless you can produce a paper—a polished, thorough paper that displays the months' effort that we've trusted you to put into it—by tonight, I'll have to take your case to the academic board, where they will consider putting you on probation."

The ground dropped out from under me.

"Is there anything I can do?" I asked weakly.

"I've told you several times in emails this week and last. Unless you can send me a copy of your paper tonight, I can't do anything for you." His eyebrows contracted; this was difficult for him. "Listen, confidentially, I'll let you submit a rough draft. But it has to express the thesis you outlined to me in January, no messing around. I'll tell the board I'm reviewing it, and I'll give you a week to get a polished copy to me."

"I can't," I moaned. "I lost the whole thing. All I have are my notes."

"I'm sorry," Charlemagne said again. "I really am sorry to be the bearer of this news to you. But there's nothing else I can do for you. I can't support a shadow student. There has to be some material. And frankly, there's little excuse not to have *some* draft, partial or otherwise, of your work backed up. With the internet and thumbdrives and the library's resources, I've had students who have worked for weeks after a crash using only the public computing stations. That defense just doesn't hold water."

Now I was the one apologizing. With a rush of shame I felt the backs of my eyelids prickling. After an awkward pause, I asked myself, *Do I really have the nerve to bring up Joe Creekman?* But I couldn't bring myself to let down Bulfinch, too.

I took a deep breath and launched into my other question. I described the page briefly to my advisor and asked him if the story or the name Joe Creekman rang any bells.

"I'm not sure I've ever heard of a Joseph Creekman in academe, but I'll ask my colleagues," he said. "As to the book, it might be helpful if I could take a look at the page itself. I read a great deal of these anthology source-translation books as an undergrad, when I was still finding my sea legs with Latin. Not all of us have the gift for languages like you do," he said. His eyes twinkled.

"I don't have the book anymore," I said quickly. "I lost it." I had a solid feeling that if I told him the truth about what happened to the page, the discussion would be over.

Even my fib seemed to have a negative effect on my chances of being taken seriously. Charlemagne's gaze diverted from my face to the surface of his desk as he said in measured tones, "Hm. Well. I would like to encourage you to pursue all of your intellectual curiosities, but it sounds like you may have set yourself on a chase of the proverbial untamed waterfowl. I would strongly suggest you focus your efforts on your Abelard thesis for now. I'll ask around about your other questions, but I'd like to see some effort on your part in return."

I mumbled my goodbye and stumbled out of the office. It was clear that my advisor thought I was crazy.

❧

"How long will it take for your professor to inquire about our topic?" Bulfinch asked when I related a truncated version of the events to him.

"I'm not sure," I gulped. "Maybe about a week," I lied.

"Excellent. In the meantime, I suggest we follow other angles," he said. "Ascertain if there are any possible family connections to this Joe Creekman."

"I don't want to do that yet," I told him. I didn't want to tell him it was because my obsession with the Letter was the only secret I had been able to reliably keep from Uncle Alvin during my whole adolescence. "I don't want to inspire anyone to ask for the letter back. Not in its current condition."

Bulfinch seemed perplexed by my reluctance, but he didn't push the matter. Gathering a few books from my parents' collection, I told Bulfinch I had to leave to write a paper. He asked what it was on and I described my thesis regarding Peter Abelard's *Sic et Non*. I was examining the academic reception of Abelard's major philosophic writings from the time of his death to the present.

"See, especially after his death, his philosophic work tended to be overshadowed by his romance with Heloise. It was a trend that outlasted chivalric love, outlasted the Romantics, and remains even despite the progress of intellectual historians to examine his work today," I explained.

"Well of course," Bulfinch exclaimed. "People love a good story."

"That's part of it," I spluttered, "But it's more complicated than that. I've done a lot of research. The second half of my paper, the one that really gets down to business, the part that I think really says what I'm getting at, is all about the fall of neo-scholasticism to the forerunners of postmodern thought, and how this coincided with the debunkment of the more embellished versions of Peter and Heloise's love letters and a new burst of more faithful renditions..."

I trailed off in the face of Bulfinch's stunned expression. I was about to slink away to write twenty-five pages on the obvious, in one night, when Bulfinch begged to come with me—he longed to learn more about the customs and organization of the modern library. To tell the truth, I was relieved. I could use his help. I had no idea how I had done it the first time.

People love a good story.

And I, of all people, had needed to ask why?

CHAPTER SEVENTEEN

#312: Message Pad
Dimensions: 5" x 7"
Description: Brand new, never used. Purchased by my
mother one New Year when she decided to get
organized.

BULFINCH AND I fell asleep at the library that night. That was how I missed Professor Charlemagne's call.

Uncle Alvin had picked up instead. When I dragged myself home at eleven the next morning, he was waiting in the kitchen and I had just enough time to shove Bulfinch into the bushes before shutting the front door casually.

"School called," Uncle Alvin said without preamble as I tried to slip casually down the hall. I stopped and turned toward him, confused.

"What about?" I called back.

"It was some professor," Alvin continued. "He was expecting a rather important piece of work from you."

My heart dropped to the floor. I kicked it along in front of me as I shuffled toward the kitchen and stood in the door.

"He said he thought he'd call to check on your progress since your home computer is broken," Uncle Alvin finished. "What's going on?"

I opened my mouth, but nothing came out.

"I thought you were going to the library today," I squeaked.

"This isn't humorous to me," Uncle Alvin glowered. "Your professor didn't give me any details, but it sounds like you missed a very important deadline."

"Oh, it's just like you always told me, that school stuff doesn't matter," I tried to laugh it off.

"I never told you that," Uncle Alvin snapped back. He sighed. "I think I may have seriously misled you. I always worked hard to make sure you were intellectually independent, that you didn't allow your instincts to be tampered with by professors who have other agendas," he said. It sounded dangerously like Uncle Alvin was criticizing himself, and it made me feel even worse. "But if you choose this academic life for yourself, it's your duty to make yourself successful at it; otherwise you're wasting your time and our money."

I swayed. As curmudgeonly as Uncle Alvin could be, he rarely reprimanded me like that.

"Now tell me," he said, "How did your computer break?"

"I dropped it," I lied.

"When?"

"Last week."

"Why didn't you tell me?"

I paused a little.

"I wanted to see if IT could fix it," I fibbed again, hoping he hadn't checked my room after the phone call, even though in seven years Uncle Alvin had never entered my room without asking.

"And what is this paper?" he continued to probe.

"The first chapters of my thesis. I lost it with my computer, and I had to rewrite it last night. That's where I was," I added quickly before he could ask. "I was at the library rewriting my thesis."

"And that's all squared away?" Alvin prompted.

"Mmm-hmm," I squeaked.

"Then this ... Professor Charlemagne had better check his electronic mailbox more frequently, because he seems to have missed it this morning."

I squeaked my assent again. I felt another stab of guilt in confirming this lie against one of the only professors I'd ever known who actually replied to emails promptly.

"Was someone with you outside?" Uncle Alvin asked. "Is there anyone you'd like to invite in?"

"Oh, no," I covered. "That was just my friend, Max. She walked me home."

"Max. Is this the person you had over earlier?"

I searched my mind and remembered my earlier slip.

"Yeah, yes," I said.

"And who is this Max?" Uncle Alvin continued.

"Max is just a friend," I said. "Max no one. Just forget I ever mentioned her."

"Max is a girl?"

I dashed up the stairs, acting like I couldn't hear Uncle Alvin anymore. I was so distraught that I didn't even remember until I opened the attic door and saw Joachim that I had yet to devise a way to sneak Bulfinch into the house. I crept back downstairs, out the back door, and around the house to the front, where Bulfinch was waiting obediently behind the rhododendrons, before I looked in the kitchen window and realized Alvin was gone. I saw a fresh note fluttering on the table near where he had sat.

Uncle Alvin wasn't that easy to shake, however. I didn't bother reading his note, so I didn't realize he had only gone out for groceries (a highly unusual pastime anyway) instead of to the Peabody Library for his daily dose of cool air and musty scholarship.

I was back in the kitchen when he came in, so it was impossible to avoid him. I was washing the dishes I'd brought up to the attic—I found a few extra already up there, but I wrote that off to my forgetfulness. To my overwhelming surprise, Alvin entered with brown bags full of vegetables, cereal, and fresh fruit—all things I had assumed he was allergic to.

"What are these for?" I asked, picking up a bunch of bananas. "They'll just go bad before we can eat them all."

"Maybe you can give some to your friend Max," Alvin said significantly.

I just raised my eyebrows and shook it off.

"Rosie," he began, using my pet name, "I haven't pried into Detective Harrison's investigation because I wanted to respect your privacy. He asked me a few questions, but when he offered to fill me in on the results of his work, I told him I would wait to hear what you chose to share with me. They're your parents, and I thought you deserved to be the keeper of their story."

I stopped shifting groceries, though he continued puttering the kitchen with typical Alvin absentminded nonchalance.

"It's been a few days now, and it's difficult to ignore your efforts to avoid me. I wanted you to know this so you understand that the privilege of stewarding your parents' legacy also comes with responsibility. Your parents may be sacred to you, but I am your mother's brother and I loved her very much. You should remember that when you decide how much of the investigation you want to share with me."

I looked hard at Uncle Alvin as he shuffled around the kitchen. It was difficult to ascertain whether he longed for me to tell him more, or to shield him from the truth, or both. This moment of power was disorienting. I wanted to talk about something else. I was sick of letting people down, and sick of being let down, and I didn't want to be the bearer of Detective Harrison's news—I didn't want this new responsibility Uncle Alvin had heaped on me. I thought of Professor Charlemagne's reproach. I thought of Bulfinch waiting in the attic, trusting me entirely to give our research my best effort. And I realized that if there was a single person I couldn't tolerate the thought of disappointing anymore, it was Bulfinch in all his naïve encouragement of me. I knew now how I could steer Uncle Alvin away from the truth about my parent, and further my search at the same time.

"I don't know much," I told him, "But Detective Harrison mentioned a Joe Creekman. Do you know anything about him?"

Alvin didn't speak right away, but it was clear the name registered very strongly with him. His face became ashen, and he looked saddened and confused.

"Joseph Creekman was a college classmate of mine," he said. "I don't see how he could possibly be involved. He and your mother must have met, oh, three times in her life. And that was before she met your father. I don't think she'd even remember him if you mentioned his name."

I felt an electric thrill. Joe Creekman was real. My head spun. The impossible was materializing before my very eyes. The non-existent Joe Creekman had come to life, and there he had been, sitting in Uncle Alvin's mental

Catalogue all along. Unless this was just another dead-end, like Beauview Drive....

"Do you know how to reach him?" I asked. "If he knows anything at all, I'd like to talk to him. Just for closure."

Uncle Alvin's brow wrinkled.

"Creekman is a recluse," he said. "Doesn't like phone calls. No internet. When he still wrote academically, he used a pseudonym to deflect attention away from himself, left no trace of any 'Joe Creekman' in his schools' records. He won't even receive mail directly. Once, when he was between agents, I let him use your parents' house as a forwarding address. You were just an infant and I was living with your parents to help."

Alvin got up and rooted through the dust-coated kitchen desk. He uncovered an ancient Rolodex, which he shuffled through interminably (I wondered if it was in any kind of order) until he emerged with a yellowed card covered with many crossings-out.

"The last I heard from him, about five years ago," Alvin reported, "he had just hired an old friend to be his latest agent. He lives in Norway, and all his mail comes through her. Vita Oppenheimer."

CHAPTER EIGHTEEN

#173: The Little Book of Chess
Dimensions: 2" x 4"
Description: A summer obsession, burned out quickly.

MY HEART HAMMERED. I was so close to unraveling it all, I could almost smell the book. Joe Creekman *and* Vita had landed in my world. After Alvin gave me Vita's contact information, I mumbled something vague and slipped up to share the news with Bulfinch.

When I entered the attic, I was shocked, stunned dead in my tracks. My jaw dropped. My head spun. Something highly unusual and unexpected was going on.

Bulfinch and Joachim were getting along.

Actually, they were playing chess. Earlier that week I had excavated an old board, orphaned of its pieces, in the detritus of my attic library, and I had supplemented it with a set that I found in the Museum, an old collection of reproductions of the Lewis Chessmen that one of Uncle Alvin's distant relatives had given to him. I had smuggled the whole thing up to the attic in the hope that Bulfinch and I could go head to head one quiet afternoon. I had tingled with curiosity about medieval methods of playing the game, and I had looked forward to him teaching me his rules, assuming without question that he would be a good player.

Instead, from what I could tell of the state of the board and the burgeoning pile of conquered pieces by Joachim's elbow, Bulfinch was being walloped. And it seemed to have improved Joachim's mood a great deal.

I stepped in just in time to watch as Joachim placed his knight with finality on Bulfinch's side of the board. The game appeared to be over. Bulfinch sighed through his nose while Joachim plucked his opponent's last pieces from the board with glee, juggling them lightly above his head. Well, at least he wasn't a sore winner.

I had to smile at Bulfinch's almost comical disappointment. Even when he traveled to the future, he couldn't escape the taunts of that pack of bratty frat boys, chivalry.

I thought I would cheer him up by sharing the news of my latest discovery. For once, Joachim didn't shoot irritated glances at us for speaking in the Latin he didn't understand; instead, he continued to amuse himself juggling more and more of the chessmen at a time while striding around the room humming some verses in Old German that I could only guess were a lively tale of chivalric triumph.

The eager smile that lighted up Bulfinch's face when I told him I had finally tracked down the originator of the Letter nearly erased all of the anxiety and disappointment I had felt earlier.

"So our Joseph Creekman's agent Vita Oppenheimer will provide us with the book from which she sent him a page years ago," he said. "And then you will read the rest of the story of the knight who was misplaced and whatever miracle brought us here through the magical book will send us back."

I nodded. My gaze drifted back to Joachim, who was now looking at us while he juggled and grinning for what must be a different reason, with a significant glance at Bulfinch.

"How did you convince him to play chess with you?" I asked the erstwhile novice. "I thought he feared your holy wrath. Why'd you let him win?"

"Ha, well," he squeaked uncomfortably. "As you know, there is little to divert the non-reader in your aerie. And while I was happily occupied, my roommate was not, and I sensed that in his boredom he began to suspect a lack of evidence for my purported supernatural abilities. As you know, it is this belief that keeps him safely under our control."

I nodded, my face falling, realizing that Bulfinch was wending his way toward something less than pleasing.

"So, I knew that as most young men of his errant profession, he would be a player of chess, being, as it were, a small-scale version of his life's pursuit. In that spirit, I challenged him to a tournament. Until that tournament is complete, he is obligated to stay here as my prisoner and pay to you and myself all the dues of civility expected of an honor-bound knight awaiting ransom. If I win, then he remains in our power and my superior prowess confirms to him that it is the will of God that he obey my rules."

"And if *he* wins?"

"If he wins, I clearly am not the ... gifted individual he believes me to be. And my breach of trust releases him from captivity. At which point he will have the right to pillage and burn the home of his captors." Bulfinch gulped. "In as chivalrous a manner as possible."

I took a deep breath.

"Why did you do this?"

"As I said, I needed to occupy his mind so he wouldn't resort to violent departure earlier, if left to reflect too long on his waning fear of me."

I put my head in my hands.

"How long does the tournament last?"

"It is done when he has defeated me in a daily match for ten consecutive days."

"Ten days?! We have ten days to find a book that might not exist so we can return you to your home, or this maniac will burn and pillage mine?"

"You could put it like that."

"Ten days? Why didn't you make it longer?"

"I didn't think he'd be so good at chess!" Bulfinch sank further into his seat. "It seemed like a fantastic idea at the time. I think I read a story like that once."

✎✎

The next day when Uncle Alvin was out again—it was getting hot in the house and the Peabody Library called to him—I picked up the yellowed Rolodex card he had retrieved during our conversation, and I called Vita Oppenheimer at her agency.

It was an interminable British number. I listened to the rings, which sounded like underwater gurgles a long way away. I sat tensely at the kitchen desk, coiling the phone cord around my fingers until it pinched, wondering what Vita's voice would sound like. Finally, after two dozen rings, someone picked up.

"Kenwith, Kenwith, Fallows, Monmouth, Newton, and Oppenheimer," a young male voice chimed in crisp RP. "Peter speaking. How may I help you?"

"I'm looking for Vita Oppenheimer," I said timidly.

"May I ask who is calling?"

"She won't know me," I blurted. I corrected myself while smacking my forehead silently. "I mean, I'm a family friend. Or she's a friend of my family. She represents a guy who went to school with my uncle."

"Your father's brother or your mother's brother?" the voice asked coolly.

"My mother's brother," I explained before I realized he was mocking me.

"Please wait one moment while I see if Ms. Oppenheimer is available," he oozed, and I was subjected to a blast of crackly hold music. After five minutes I put the phone down on the desk, where I could still hear Beethoven buzzing through the earpiece. I wondered if Peter had stopped on his way back from Vita's office to make a cup of tea. Or to read *Great Expectations*. All the way through.

Finally, he picked up again, and I snatched the phone back to my ear.

"Ms. Oppenheimer cannot take your call at this time. Would you like to leave her a message?" His tone was silky, and I doubted he would even lift a finger to write down a message. I only had one chance to make this right. No fibs, no excuses.

"Listen, a long time ago Joseph Creekman, Vita's client, used my uncle to forward his mail. Years after my uncle moved out of our house, my family received a letter from Vita—er, Ms. Oppenheimer—to Mr. Creekman containing a page from a book. Would you please tell Ms. Oppenheimer that I have her letter, and that it's very important that I speak to her about it?"

"Peter, you may hang up," I heard a mature female voice on the line. "I will speak to this young lady."

"Yes, ma'am," Peter said, sounding significantly less important, and I heard the click of a phone disconnecting.

"I hope you don't mind Peter," the female voice continued. "He was only doing his job. He's still in training, and I thought I'd listen in to see what this call was really about. Of course you can excuse me for being reluctant to speak to someone with a connection so far-fetched."

I was bowled over, so at first I just let the woman patter on agreeably while I composed myself. I felt a surge of relief for being believed, proving myself trustworthy for once.

"Thanks," I breathed. "I appreciate it."

"To be frank, I'm actually delighted to hear from a relative of Alvin's. He's such a peculiar fellow, he rarely picks up the phone himself. He's a little like Joe in that regard." Vita took a deep breath. "Is he doing well?"

"Yes, yes," I told her, unable to think of anything else to share about my solemn, sedentary uncle. She didn't seem to require effusive response, however—her pleasure at being reconnected to this piece of her past poured out of her in story. I only had to hang on and listen and prompt her gently. It sounded like she had been waiting a long time for someone to recount this tale to.

"We value our clients' privacy a great deal. I'm more than a literary agent to Joe. He's an old and dear friend, and he wishes for nothing more than to isolate himself from the trials and traumas of everyday life. As Alvin is well aware, Joe is delicate ... mentally, and for five years now I've been the mediator between him and the world."

I explained to Vita the story of the Letter, how I had received it when I was twelve, how my mother and I had tried to find its home, and how we'd eventually opened it.

"We never thought to ask Uncle Alvin about it back then," I said. "He had never mentioned using us as a forwarding address anyway, and my mom had never seen anything arrive for Joe Creekman before. Alvin himself said she wouldn't have even remembered meeting him, it was so long ago that she did."

"From what I've heard and seen of Joe's small, eccentric band of friends," Vita replied laughingly, "It's not surprising your uncle neglected a minor detail like informing your family of his use of your address."

I continued the story, telling her frankly about how I had kept the Letter a secret from Alvin for years for selfish reasons until curiosity resurfaced as an adult. I had a strong desire to speak truthfully to this woman, who, in only a few minutes on a muddy phone connection, had managed to remind me of my mother. The only lie was one of omission—I couldn't possibly tell her about Bulfinch or the knight ... or the page's mysterious erasure.

"It sounds like you've been through a lot, young lady," Vita said. "And so has my little piece of correspondence. I never wondered why Joe hadn't written back—he is a beautiful letter-writer when he finds the inclination, which is extremely rare—and later, when Joe hired me and I discovered the ancient error in my little black address book, I assumed it was long lost by that time."

"The funny thing is," I replied, "You wrote the wrong address, but it still came to the right place—just too late. Uncle Alvin moved out again when I was really little, and Joe Creekman must not have told everybody to change his forwarding address. So my mom and I got it instead."

"That's very much like Joe," Vita laughed. "It takes him years to make the tiniest adjustments." She sighed. "Back then, he was still able to do most of it on his own, if it occurred to him. After sending him that letter and waiting indefinitely for a response, I began to worry about him. But then I met my husband, moved back to London, and tacked my name onto the end of a venerable literary agency, and that anxiety for Joe was swept under a rug. About five years ago I looked up your uncle out of curiosity, since he was the last point of contact I remember linking the world to Joe. That's when he corrected the address I had used so long ago and told me Joe wasn't doing very well. He had had a mental breakdown in Georgia and was let go from the college where he taught there."

Vita sounded softly melancholy as she related the story, as if the pain had faded to a weak streak of blue in the past.

"I had been very fond of Mr. Creekman when I had encountered him for the first time at that university, years before," she continued, "And I longed to do what I could to help him in this difficult period of his life. At that time, your uncle was his closest counselor and friend, and he told me Joe desperately longed to set himself up in a secluded spot close to the sites of the history he loved so well, to dedicate himself without interruption to a life of independent scholarship."

I scanned my personal timeline for that period. I'd been a precocious, friendless undergrad at Loyola. I'd had no idea that at the time Uncle Alvin was managing the affairs of a troubled friend hundreds of miles away.

"Well, I have nothing but respect for your uncle, and his efforts were noble, but it was clear that he was barely better equipped to confront the practical concerns of Joe's dissolving career than Joe was able to care for himself," Vita told me. "And Alvin already had you to look after. He only spoke of you and your pursuits in the highest terms. He's a very proud guardian, you know."

I hadn't known.

"So I stepped up to help our friend out of the snares that plagued him," Vita continued. "In the official capacity,

I was his agent, representing his works to publishers and defending his legal concerns. But I gave him much more attention than any normal client. By that time, Joe had a severe phobia of telephones, computers, televisions, and other electronics. It was as if his mind insisted on a pre-twentieth-century existence. I took him into my home at first. My husband had just left me, and I actually craved the thought of taking care of someone other than myself." She sounded wistful. "Joe insisted on crossing the Atlantic by boat.

"He stayed with me until I could find a suitable place for him and arrange all of his communications to be channeled through me. He had enough family money saved to serve him comfortably through life in a small, secluded community in Germany. I was sad to see him go, but even more saddened to see him so ... reduced, as he was after his illness in Georgia. Where once had been an alert, if eccentric ... an affectionate, if retiring ... a highly intelligent, if absentminded man, was now a shadow. All day and night all he would speak about was the fourteenth century. It was difficult to determine if the details about the home I was preparing for him even penetrated his mind. He would only sign the papers to commit ... to his new residence after looking over photos of the ruined medieval abbey on the mountain above it.

"During the first few months, I heard from the management of his community that several times he had to be fetched from the great abandoned halls on the mountain because he had mistaken the abbey for his home. It became clear that he never stayed long enough to endanger his health in bad weather, and he always returned peacefully, so eventually they just set up a cot with some blankets and other supplies up there to await his visits, and sent a caretaker up to check on him every so often if he wasn't heard from in the village for more than a day."

I took a deep breath.

"Why did you send him that page from a book so long ago?" I asked.

I could hear the smile in her voice.

"Oh, that. Yes, now I remembered why you called. I'm sorry for subjecting you to that rather extended story. Yes, the letter. I still remember it. I had been clearing out my desk in preparation to move when I found my old school papers. Between two issues of the journal we had edited together so many years ago, I found that page. It had fallen out of a book he had been reading once before a meeting. I had noticed it on the ground, and on a girlish impulse I had wanted to preserve it. Well, upon finding it again years later, I thought it would be amusing to send it back, as a way of getting back in touch. As you know, that attempt was an unmitigated failure."

"But there wasn't any note inside," I pressed.

"There wasn't? I remember I tore a strip of paper out of one of my notebooks and wrote, *Remember me?* with my address."

I thought of the tear near the corner of the envelope that had fascinated me so much.

"It must have slipped out," I told her. "The envelope was torn when we got it."

"Haha, well, I suppose it's unimportant considering he would never have seen it in the first place," she chuckled. "Did you read the story on it?"

"Of course!" I cried. "I loved it. It lit up my childhood. It's the reason I study history."

"It's quite a captivating little tale," Vita agreed. "I used to lie in bed for hours, imagining the ending."

I glowed with the discovery that someone else felt exactly the way I did about the page. I nearly gave in to the impulse to share the whole tale with Vita, to tell her that the story's hero and his chronicler were now living in my attic. But I was afraid that if I spilled something so outlandish, she would only assume that I was in the same mental state as her friend Joe Creekman.

"So you don't know what book it's from?" I asked. "I was hoping you would be able to tell me so I could look up the ending."

"Oh, I know what book it's from," she replied. "It's a very unique book. I wouldn't forget it. But I never asked Joe to see it because I didn't want to know the rest of the story, however much there was left. I rather preferred to imagine it myself.

"It's a very rare book—there was a short run of it before the publisher went out of business for a variety of oversights, both academic and financial. It's not surprising when you look at the book, since they printed the page numbers on the wrong side, among other eccentricities. Joe knew one of the editors, however, and he prized his copy. He was the only person I've known in the world that I've seen reading it. I can ask him to lend you his copy if you'd like."

"I would," I replied. "I would like that very much."

"Right, then I'll call you again when I receive it from him. Still live with your uncle in Baltimore?"

"Yes."

"Then I'll speak to you later. Take care of Alvin."

I told her I'd try, and I didn't tell her who else I'd be taking care of in the meantime.

I had been nervous about the glacial rate at which communications traveled between Alvin's friends, judging by their history, but I was relieved to hear from Vita again after Joachim's third consecutive win at the daily chess match. She had sent Joe a telegram. I hadn't even known telegrams still existed. She told me it was the most reliable way to make him respond in a timely manner; most operators would ask for a return message upon delivery. He did have the book, and he would send it via Vita. If Joachim's winning streak continued, we had one week for the book to arrive and perform a second miracle before his restless medieval violence was unchained.

All I have to do is keep them quiet upstairs, I thought. Then Uncle Alvin came home. I heard him calling my name from the living room, and I ran down to him, perplexed since he usually waited to bump into me if he had anything to share.

"Are you hiding a boy from me?" he asked abruptly, as I skidded into the room. I nearly fell over.

"What?" I cried. "Hiding a boy? In this house?"

He paused, as if that wasn't the response he had expected, and I kicked myself mentally.

"Well, do you bring someone into this house? Someone I don't know about?" he prompted. "What about this Max?"

"Max is a girl!" I blurted before I realized that was irrelevant.

"You've been acting very unusual lately," he steamrolled on, "And I don't like it."

"Well, big news, I can act however I want," I whined at him.

"I also received a very unusual call from the phone company today. They tell me we've exceeded our long distant minutes and will be subject to some not insubstantial charges."

"They must have us mixed up with a neighbor," I said. "You should call them back."

"Far be it from me to intrude on your life, you're an adult," he continued, "but since we share this house, there are things I must know."

"I thought you said it was my house too," I said, going back in my mind to the day Alvin had discovered my attic Catalogue project. I wanted to frighten him off the subject with his own words, to sting. It didn't even land.

"You may have a friend, and I'm pleased if that entertains you," he continued in his authoritative tone, as if he were distinctly unentertained. "But the idea that you would sneak around me, it's unacceptable."

"Who do you think I snuck up there?" I said. "There's no one. It's just me."

"I wouldn't presume to intrude on your privacy and spy on your whereabouts and company," Uncle Alvin towered, getting up, "But if you don't tell me now if you've brought any person into this house and deliberately concealed him, I will consider it a grave breach of trust."

"I haven't done anything!" I called after him as he lumbered out of the kitchen. "There's no one there," I said, and I wasn't sure if I directed the words at him or myself.

I stayed a little longer after he had gone, contemplating the surface of the kitchen table, pinned down as if my limbs were lead. Then, carried up by a second wind of righteous indignation, I swept out to the patio, where I slammed the back door hard enough I hoped Alvin would hear it.

Loitering in the shade of the bushes at the edge of the garden wall was someone I hadn't seen in what felt like a long time—the fabled Max. I wasn't expecting her, though it made perfect sense for her to slink back into my daily existence just when things became almost too much to bear. Just as naturally, I immediately began to vent as she slid toward me in the dizzying twilight.

"He knows," I told her. "He asked me if I was hiding a boy in the house. He knows someone's up there, and he's just playing with me to make me nervous. He always does things like that to teach me some childish lesson about responsibility, to make me admit how stupid I'm being before he tells me so."

"That doesn't prove anything," Max replied, easing herself into a patio chair and throwing her legs up on the little round table that matched it. "He knows you're keeping something secret, but that's pretty obvious. You're the worst person at keeping secrets I've ever known. What he doesn't know is that what you're keeping secret might be imaginary."

"No," I began, but the word dragged hesitantly in my mouth and Max smirked. I was stuck, even in the friendship that gave me comfort and escape, between what I wanted and what was real. If Max was right and Uncle Alvin was on the wrong scent and my visitors existed only in my mind, then at least I was free from fear of discovery or responsibility. But I didn't want to settle for my own imagination—I wanted them to be real so much it made my stomach ache and the back of my skull tingle with a weird electric thrill.

Allison had seen them both, I told myself. But what if Allison was just in my head? What if she was just like ... I had to stop myself. I couldn't question the reality of every person who befriended me. Allison was in my class, and there she spoke at great length with the professor for the enlightenment of us all, and the professor seemed to have innate and unwavering faith in the reality of the girl sitting in his front row. I calmed myself down, wondering at Max's ability to knock down everything I believed in like so many card houses. I had seen the knight and his chronicler, I had touched them, I had smelled them, and the only way to convince me they weren't real would be a diagnosis of total mental collapse.

"I know he knows," I said finally, with a sternness that made Max's eyebrows fall. "He knows everything. I don't know how. Actually, it probably wasn't that hard. It just can't be accidental, all the things he said. Maybe he doesn't know anything else, but he knows I've got someone up there."

"Okay, then," she shrugged and got up. "I'm just saying. Maybe you're both crazy. Or should I say, all four of you." As she was about the slip fluidly through the clinging brambles between our backyard and the next, hoisting herself up on the wall by a tree branch, she looked back and said, "I just came to show you this." Out of her back pocket she slipped a crumpled piece of paper, unfolding it enough for me to peek at what was printed on it. Almost instantly, I recognized the size and shape of the text on the page, the familiar paragraph breaks, the mismatched heading sizes—it was the Letter from seven years ago, my letter, the one that had been wiped clean by the knight's arrival.

I didn't know how Max had gotten it, though she'd proven herself capable of sneaking into things when I wasn't around. What I didn't understand or try to understand or need to understand was how the writing had reappeared; at that moment, all I knew was that I wanted it, that every atom in my brain screamed for it, to touch it, to read it again. But as quickly as Max had shown it to me from across the yard, she dropped down on the other side of the wall and disappeared. I ran into the alley. I couldn't see her anywhere. I ran down the block, I looked behind dumpsters, I skinned my elbows hoisting myself up on the garden walls of my neighbors to see if Max was hiding in their yards, but she was nowhere. Once I had lost sight of her, she had ceased to exist, and she had taken the page with her.

I couldn't hold it in, I screamed for her aloud.

"Max!" I called. "I hate you, get back here," my voice cracked.

After the sound of my voice the alley was densely still. I heard a few back doors creak and I realized, feeling a prickle along my back, that I was being watched from several upstairs windows.

Then I heard a more pronounced clatter and Uncle Alvin emerged into the alley, looking haggard and concerned.

"Rosie, what the hell is going on?" he grunted as he jogged toward me. To see him break out of his usual amble and push himself to move faster made him seem about a decade older, and I was overwhelmed by how frail he looked, teetering to my rescue.

"I don't know," I replied weakly. I groped for an explanation while Uncle Alvin stared at me with a mixture of relief and irritation.

"Was someone trying to hurt you?" he asked. "What happened?"

"I—I was—a dog chased me," I said. "He lives down the street, I think."

Uncle Alvin stared at me hard for a long half a minute. I thought I felt the skeptical gaze of three other neighbors from cracked back doors at the same time. Then Uncle Alvin seemed to reach a conclusion that left me feeling distinctly lousy and stupid.

"Next time you see him, don't run away," Uncle Alvin told me. "If you run from a dog, he'll want to chase you."

Uncle Alvin waited for me to come with him back to our house, and when we crossed through our little gate again, Alvin relocked it deliberately. I took the hint, but I couldn't come into the house just yet, so I stood pretending to look at the budding lily of the valley that crowded in the shade of the back wall until he went inside and I was alone. I sank into the same patio chair that Max had left, and I noticed I was shaking.

I floated there in between time and now until a flicker caught my eye—the attic light, which I hadn't noticed go on, had blinked out again.

With a new sense that events would resolve themselves if each evening arrived with the graceful serenity of those summer nights, I crept up to the attic, to the two men I hid there. I stayed up all night while I told Bulfinch in whispers about the explorers and artists of the Renaissance, while he fed me stories about the castles and knights surrounding his home.

CHAPTER NINETEEN

#68: Hidey Box
Dimensions: 8" x 12" x 8"
Description: Small box with a false bottom for concealing even smaller items.

THE NEXT DAY when I came downstairs, Uncle Alvin was raising dust in the living room. The air was so mottled with it at first that it was hard to tell what he was doing, and conditioned as I was to the mustiness of the house, I was overtaken by a coughing fit.

My eyes closed and watering, I felt Alvin press a water glass into my hand and I took a sip, calming the tickle in my throat. When I opened my eyes, he had already shuffled back to his work in the corner of the room where he kept his favorite books, the Virgil and Ovid and Pope and the two dozen other volumes that he paged through almost daily. I crept up behind him to watch what he was doing there.

On the floor, a box contained most of the first shelf's collection. The dust was agitated by a feather duster that Alvin yielded halfheartedly on the back of the case, the far corners and the little pockets of spaces that had been sealed by the habitual order of the books. I didn't think those nooks had seen sunlight for twenty years at least.

"What's going on?" I asked, fixated on the gaping empty shelf like a missing tooth in someone's grin.

"It's all going upstairs," Alvin replied. "I'd appreciate it if you would lend a hand." He slid the box toward me, but only a few centimeters before he turned back to filling a second box with the next shelf's contents.

"Where upstairs?" I asked, confused, hoisting up the box automatically—it was a habit ingrained from my early teens.

"Rosie, use your brain," he snapped without looking at me. I stood for a moment, taken aback, but when he refused to turn to me, I took the box upstairs to the only place he could have meant—the third-story Museum, just below my attic.

I left the box on the landing and peered up the narrow stairway to my hideout. The door was ajar. Tossing a glance over my shoulder to make sure Alvin wasn't spying, I darted up to the study. I lowered my eyes, adjusting to the brightness flooding through the windows at the top of the house. What I could see was a terror—two silhouettes clashed with weapons, emitting a series of muffled bumps, crashes, and grunts. I rushed forward.

"Stop this!" I cried, hanging onto Bulfinch's arm. "What's going on?"

Bulfinch, panting happily, dropped the broomstick he was holding, and Joachim, just as good-naturedly, lowered his sword.

"Oh, our knight here was just teaching me some of the fundamentals of chivalric prowess," Bulfinch beamed. "Excellent physical invigoration, especially during our unfortunately necessary confinement. Wouldn't like to pursue it as a career. I have to say, though, it's quite more diverting than I'd thought when my parents sent me out to page as a young boy."

"I thought you'd stayed home all your childhood," I queried.

"Oh. That. Well, there might have been a short time when I very briefly dabbled in knighthood, but found it wasn't to my taste."

"You got sent back," I concluded flatly.

"One could say. But my dear mother had nothing but the strongest encouragement for my scholarly path. And I must agree with her choice of my profession since I have trouble enough watching a novice whipped, much less the ability to slay a man. Though one must admit," he said, swaggering with his elbow on the table, "I would make quite a figure on a palfrey with banners."

I couldn't suppress a snort, but I still swam in the urgency of my task.

"You have to keep quiet," I warned them. "And keep the door shut at all times. My uncle is moving his study to the floor directly below you, and I'm afraid he may be catching on."

Bulfinch paled.

"We only sparred because we assumed he was gone, as you told me he usually is at this time," Bulfinch whispered. "I hadn't seen nor heard anything from below until you came."

I sighed.

"Well, at least he didn't walk in on your training," I murmured. I sensed my time was running out before Uncle Alvin would start to wonder where I was.

My heart pounding, I climbed downstairs for the second box.

That was how most of the morning went. With each box, it was as if Alvin were saying, "You know why I'm moving upstairs. Now will you tell me?" I had planned on going to class, but the rhythmic chore was mesmerizing and wiped away the scream of anticipation I felt when I thought about facing Professor Charlemagne's dashed expectations again. I'd almost rather drop out.

We ate lunch together, silently, Uncle Alvin and I.

When we went back to work afterwards, I tried to pry into the change without sounding defensive or petulant.

"You won't be comfortable upstairs," I said. "You can move everything else, but your chair is still down here."

"We're taking the furniture up tomorrow."

"We can't fit your chair up the stairwell! Anyway, you shouldn't be moving things that heavy."

"I see, my health and safety happily coincide with your wishes."

I heaved a sigh and left him, lugging an old record player. When I got back, he had nearly done filling a crate with his favorite records, and a few I didn't recognize that must have been lost behind the stack until now.

"Put all these next to Grandma Ethel's divan and set the player up."

Grandma Ethel's divan was in the first room off the landing, with a clear view of the stairs up to the attic. The next day, I arrayed small ottoman and two square tables around it, and they were quickly heaped upon with stacks of relocated books.

That afternoon, Detective Harrison called.

"The news is good and bad," he said, gently. "The case is closed."

I held my breath.

"We've traced most of the missing money," he said. "Whatever we couldn't track down wasn't enough for them to run away on. Without any other evidence of their intent to flee, we are reasonably confident in believing that their disappearance was unconnected with their crimes."

I released my breath. The word "crimes" stung me like a needle, but mostly I felt relief. I let it trickle into me. *"Without any other evidence of their intent to flee."*

"Unfortunately, because of a procedure called asset forfeiture, the police department will be seizing your house, as it was purchased with funds implicated in a crime."

"It's not my house anymore," I said, tonelessly. It was the first time I'd said those words, to myself or another. Yes, the house belonged to us in deed, but for years it had been someone else's home. The place I wanted back existed in my memory only.

I thanked Detective Harrison for the information and hung up. At least, I think I did; my mouth moved, and later, the phone was in its cradle. I moved as if in a dream.

I could now imagine my parents drowning quietly in a sea cave, still loving me. But my mind refused to settle on that image. Instead, it kept being drawn back to the fact that their trip took them past Bulfinch's abbey. My mind went over my mom's postcards and letters, especially her last one. Was there a clue?

❧

My resentment of Alvin intensified as I dwelled on his lack of consideration, changing everything in the house just when I needed the small comfort of knowing he was in his habitual chair, following habitual habits, holding down his corner of my life.

It appeared it would take longer than even I had expected to complete Uncle Alvin's move to the third floor. He had accumulated several decades' worth of comfort items, books, and specimens with which to surround himself, and he wouldn't adjourn upstairs until his seating arrangement was almost perfectly replicated there. For the first day, he remained downstairs, directing my traffic. I didn't loiter upstairs too much while I was helping; I didn't want anything to look suspicious. But late at night, when Alvin had gone to bed and I finally saw his light flicker out down the hall, I crept upstairs with an armful of food, when the silence of the night became dead and the streetlamps sagged under its weight.

"We need to work on your chess game," I whispered to Bulfinch. He had lost for the fourth time that day.

∽⁍⁍∽

Uncle Alvin didn't venture to the third floor the next day or the day after that. The number of items that had to be marched up there before he would settle himself was immense, and I began to wonder if it was all part of a ploy to force a confession from me before he uprooted his entire home.

Bulfinch lost the fifth and then the sixth games of chess.

When I thought about the sword hanging over me— literally, in the attic—I broke into a cold sweat, which was often. I strove to reclaim the serenity that the beauty of the evenings gave me. But in the clamor of the day, I couldn't dodge the responsibility of my active role in our game. I felt that I was holding up a sinking boat by stretching my body to plug every hole with a finger or toe.

Uncle Alvin started giving me piles of art from the walls to take upstairs. I wondered if he planned on entirely stripping the living room before he joined his things.

Bulfinch lost the seventh game of chess.

I started spending most of my nights in the attic. To be cautious, I avoided the attic entirely during the daytime. At night, I brought up as much food as I could to last the boys through the next day and let them sneak out to wash up and use the bathroom. I spent every day dreaming of the things I would discuss that night with Bulfinch, new ideas on his mystery arrival, chess tips, things that had reminded me of him throughout the day. I tried not to dwell on the continuing wait for Joe Creekman's book to arrive.

Bulfinch lost his eighth game of chess.

At night, while Joachim snoozed, Bulfinch sat with me through the small hours and told me about how he had spent his day. In whispers, he had discovered his roommate loved a good story as much as he did. Joachim respected the rules of his chess tournament with Bulfinch as well as he did because it reminded him of his favorite story, a tale about a chivalrous knight who is beseeched by his love to set aside his sword and meet his rival in battle on the board. Joachim had told him that story and then many more he knew about knights and dragons and other things Bulfinch had always thought were stupid. Bulfinch was often so wrapped up in each saga that, after his roommate was asleep and I crept into the darkened attic, he would be bursting to relate the latest episode to me. His excitement inspired comically endearing tics: his dancing eyebrows, the way his mouth turned up slightly at the corners as he worked up to an especially funny part, as if he couldn't wait until after the joke to laugh. Sometimes he reached out and grasped my hands while he talked.

To entertain the knight, Bulfinch told Joachim about the classical myths of Ovid, which Bulfinch had acquired from a private bookseller and subsequently hid from his family— it was scandalous material.

Bulfinch lost his ninth game of chess while I was still waiting for the book.

Bulfinch told me that he and Joachim used their daily game of chess to pass the time. Sometimes it took hours or a whole afternoon; they would move a few pieces, then break to take a nap. The only consistency seemed to be Joachim's victory. Sometimes between late-night stories, or during them, Bulfinch and I would play rounds of chess to give him practice. But I was such a poor player that most of the time the board pieces just became figures that Bulfinch used to illustrate his current tale.

The day after Bulfinch's ninth chess disaster, I began to wonder what life would be like after the unleashed Joachim burst out of our burning and plundered house and made his way once again into Baltimore. He'd probably wind up in jail. Then—if he decided to spare myself and Bulfinch, which was questionable—I'd have a lot of explaining to do.

I stumbled through the day in a haze of resignation, wincing at every thump, expecting Joachim's wrath to clatter down the steps at any moment. That's why I jumped three feet in the air when the doorbell rang at four that afternoon, as the sunshine goldened on the tenth day of the fateful chess tournament.

I ran to answer the front door as soon as my mind registered that the alarming sound was not a signal of impending doom. Outside, a delivery service man stood wilting on the front step, his polyblend uniform screaming discomfort.

My stunned look seemed to spark some sympathy as he asked me to sign for the package. I accepted the box mutely and shut the door.

My hands shook as I took it inside.

From the living room, Uncle Alvin called out to ask what the business was. I replied in a wavering voice that it was just something I had ordered, and I dashed upstairs.

I stopped short on the second floor, however. Instead of going immediately to my inmates, I turned into my bedroom, a place I had seen little of in the past week. Dropping the package on the bed, I then shut my door and barricaded it with a pillow to stop anyone from entering suddenly. Mostly it was for my own peace of mind.

The box was heavy for its size, and it weighed down on my comforter the same way I had imagined the Letter had dented my bedclothes when I had stared at it as a child. I approached it cautiously as if it contained a live animal. Holding my breath, I broke the tape sealing the box and lifted the top.

Neatly nested inside was a thick, squat, red hardcover book. It was worn around the edges and spine, and the corners and binding were frayed. On the cover, embossed in flaking gold, was the title:

Pars Plebotinum: A Collection of Unfinished Manuscripts
Ed. by Anderson J. T. Pickworth

I trembled. Goosebumps stood up on my arms. I was afraid to touch it, even to breathe on it. Suddenly all my desire to read the next page of Bulfinch's story drained out of me.

I thought of the competition upstairs. Had Joachim already won again today? Had they played yet?

I took a deep breath. It was time. I had to do this. *Open the book*, I told myself. *Find page 120.*

But if I read it here and now, would Bulfinch and Joachim disappear immediately? Would that be the end, plain and simple? I recoiled from the book. Not before I could say goodbye. I had to wait.

I wanted Bulfinch for one more day.

I looked forward to sharing the story of my day with him every evening. His stories ignited my imagination, and I liked how he responded to my enthusiasm with equal fire. When he smiled, I felt happy. When he was in need, I prized the ability to help him. My day was dim until I could see a smile creeping up his lips or the twitch of his ears. I didn't want to lose my only real friend.

The thought entered my mind that I could hide the book and pretend it had never come. I tried to brush it away, to hold to my resolution to fulfill my responsibilities. Before I had a chance to let the seed take root, I closed the box again, clutched it under my arm, and marched out of my room and up the stairs.

On the third-story landing, I crashed directly into Bulfinch. He pulled me aside into the first room and shut the door behind us. I was so dumbfounded that I nearly dropped the box, but my fears were allayed by Bulfinch's beaming face.

"I won," he blurted with unrestrained glee. "I was so jubilant I had to tell you immediately. I was just about to go seek you in the house. Imagine that! What if I had run into your uncle! I forgot all risk. I simply had to give you the news and share my accomplishment. We're safe, for another ten days! I won!"

He threw his arms around me spontaneously, and I returned the embrace tightly, holding on for reasons he couldn't have been able to guess.

"What's that?" he asked when his exhilaration had subsided enough for him to notice the package that had slipped out from under my arm in our hug.

"Nothing," I murmured, pushing it under a cabinet with my toe.

CHAPTER TWENTY

#192: Dream Catcher
Dimensions: 7" diameter
Description: Used to hang over my bed as a child; I
thought it would let me catch my dreams and keep
them, so they would be real.

THE BOOK WAS still hiding under the cabinet, weighing on the floor, through the ceiling above my bed. But as long as I couldn't see it, I was happy pretending it wasn't there. A leaf had turned when I realized I had the power to refuse to turn its leaves.

The next morning, I felt lighter, as if the air had cleared itself in the night.

I began to see a new future.

The games of chess could go on forever, every disaster saved in the nick of time by a chance victory by Bulfinch.

Then, the adventures we could have. The things I would tell him and the stories I'd hear. Every day, sneaking around Uncle Alvin; every night, whispering over the snoring of Joachim.

I wondered, dangerously, if these new fantasies would alter the world the way that one momentous dream had—if

I could shift reality again, if my heart glowed strongly enough. But when Bulfinch and the knight arrived in the attic, my heart had been lead and my veins cold.

I imagined my new knight, his two gray eyes alight, with a lady—not me, but someone from a Pre-Raphaelite portrait, in a shining mantle like a peacock's tail, translucent and soft, and a halo of curling bright hair, and a limpid, inward gaze. They met frequently in this pathless wood, far away from time.

A golden warmth washed over me as I sank into it. My hands steadied.

The knight met his lady in the woods and they—I had to focus to find my place again—they posed under a vine-wrapped tree. They exchanged letters, wordlessly looking at each other. Confined to letters, their love thrived safely and secretly, and they never spoke.

I remembered the comical relief on Bulfinch's face when we could finally understand each other—and I couldn't stop myself from laughing a little.

It was too hot in the living room to concentrate. The crate was nearly full, and I had lost count—I looked at the remaining shelf. Sixteen volumes more to go. And then the Catalogue Exodus would be complete.

I climbed up the stairs at half speed, groaning under the weight of the crate—all those binders added up—and the oppressive heat. I balanced the crate on the banister at the second-floor landing and flexed my fingers, feeling where the plastic had bit into them in the crook of their joints.

Like an addict, I reached for fantasy again. My hands slackened and the crate tottered—I snatched it and put it on the floor and sat on top of it, between source and destination, on the landing of the stairs.

If I stopped living mentally in the Middle Ages, I wondered, would Bulfinch disappear?

I imagined him ripped away again, for good; I imagined his absence when, a month earlier, I could only have imagined his presence. If he left now—it would feel as if I had left home, too, and been flung away to someplace incomprehensible, astray in time. The waking dream of last night rushed back to me—the moment I had seen the book and knew it could take away my friend, and as I tried to comprehend it, the aching sense of loss and the melancholy determination to wait, even though, like in nightmares, the world could have been a white room that I could see all around and still I wouldn't find him.

It was a moment like that that had brought him to me.

I wondered if I could follow him back to that place.

I was still eaten by the shame of Uncle Alvin knowing—the fear of what he might say if they met. Then I would be revealed: I had been harboring a stranger in our attic. I wanted to crawl away, with Bulfinch, somewhere hidden—a cave maybe—where I wouldn't have to explain, where we could live like teenaged runaways.

It had been a quarter past three for hours.

I hauled myself up and hoisted the crate to my hip. I pounded up the stairs, and when I turned the corner into the Museum, I saw Uncle Alvin sitting on Grandma Ethel's divan.

"Thank you, Rosie," he grunted. "That will be all for now."

My shoulders slumped. I didn't dare to even look at the attic door. Obeying a silent order, I marched down the stairs, the backs of my eyelids stinging.

Max was sitting in the window of my bedroom.

"How the hell did you get in here?" I spat at her. "And where's my letter?"

"I don't know," she answered, and for a moment I thought that was her response to both questions. "I never took it. It's still in your notebook. Go check."

"I saw you with it in the garden!"

"You're imagining things."

"What do you want?" I growled, backing against the closed door.

"I wanted to read this," she said, holding up the box containing Joe Creekman's book. She opened the top, her fingers nearly brushing the cover.

"Don't touch the *Plebotinum*!" I wailed at her, overcome by panic.

"Or what? Your precious Bulfinch will disappear?" Max taunted, but she dropped the book. She slinked off the windowsill and stepped toward me.

"That's what you want to happen, isn't it," I said, but I still shrank from her. "That's why you stole the page. That's why you tried to convince me he isn't real. You don't want to be replaced, so you want him to be just like—"

"It's only what you want," Max glowered. "You're the one hiding it from him. If this works, everything's a little too real and then—*poof!*—you've lost Bulfinch like your momma and your papa—"

"Go away," I moaned. "Why do you keep preying on me?"

"If you didn't want me around, I wouldn't be here," Max countered coolly. "I'm just telling you want you're thinking already."

"Get out."

"You're already trying to turn them into fantasy. I know. I can tell."

"Get out of my room."

"You just want to keep them up there like prisoners, to entertain you."

"Get out of my house."

"As long as you hide them, you're going to need me. I won't go away."

"Leave me!"

I heard Uncle Alvin call my name faintly upstairs. My heart leapt into my throat—had I really been that loud? I turned instinctively toward the door. Behind me, I heard Max whine, "You're no fun," but when I turned back, she was already gone.

I picked the book up from the floor, still in its box. I closed the box neatly and tucked it under my bed. Max was wrong. Bulfinch could stay forever, and everything would be alright.

I stood, determined to march up to the attic, whether Alvin was watching or not. If I was going to be defiant, I would also have to be brave.

But as I passed the third-story landing, my eyes darted to Uncle Alvin's seat. I was stopped in my tracks when I saw him, doubled over in pain.

The phone fell from his hand.

"Oh hello, Rosie," he wheezed as I walked in. "They're coming to take me to the hospital."

I ran to him.

"What's wrong? Why didn't you yell for me?" As soon as I said it, the revelation hit me and I choked back a sob.

Kneeling by him, I saw his face was very red, and a few tears streamed down his cheeks. He was gasping.

"Phone was closer," he replied.

CHAPTER TWENTY-ONE

"A MINOR HEART EVENT," the doctor called it. "Your Uncle suffers from unstable angina, which could be a sign of impending heart attack, or even its cause.

"You're lucky he recognized the symptoms as early as he did," the doctor explained to us both in the hospital room. "Some patients wait too long, thinking the early stages are just an extreme case of heartburn."

"My doctor told me I had heart disease," Uncle Alvin wheezed weakly in reply. "But I lost my prescription."

I hadn't known Uncle Alvin had heart disease. I couldn't even say when the last time he'd been to the doctor was.

After the alarming rush of the EMTs into our home and our hasty parade to the ambulance, it didn't take long to stabilize Alvin. That was the word they used. He didn't look stable to me. He looked smaller, frailer, more delicate then I'd ever seen him before.

Then there was the interminable wait in the Union Memorial emergency room. That alarmed me more than the previous rush. I wanted to see action, I wanted to see a bustling crowd of doctors like on the TV shows, everyone in the hospital gathering around to ensure Uncle Alvin would be okay. Instead, we waited in triage, then we waited in a miserable lobby, then we waited in an ER room off a crowded hall where I could still hear the coughs and snores or worse sounds from the other patients over the murmur of their visitors and nurses and television sets, and everything was drenched in the sick scent of sanitizer with a faint but just detectable undertone of urine.

Finally, after three hours, Uncle Alvin was admitted and moved to a regular overnight room. They were keeping him overnight for tests. After the doctor left, Alvin's eyes drooped to what looked like extremely welcome sleep.

He wasn't the bad guy anymore, and I realized with a crush of self-hate that he'd never been the bad guy, that he'd always been there, waiting for me to come to him. I felt as if his illness were a direct result of my neglect. I felt I deserved it if the whole world lined up to kick and slap me. My whole body longed to hug him, to show him that he was still my Uncle Alvin, but he looked so weak I was afraid it would crush him.

I didn't know what to do. I had never had this much responsibility for another person. I felt at once that I should be tearing the place apart to care for and protect him and that everything would carry on precisely as if I hadn't existed if I left the hospital now.

But I wouldn't leave—I couldn't. I wouldn't know what to do if I were away, either. And I had the overwhelming fear that if I let him out of my sight, Uncle Alvin would be disappeared by the nurses to a different part of the hospital where he would be irrecoverably lost and I would never see him again, and I wouldn't know how to live without Uncle Alvin around.

I was surrounded by the beeping and wheezing and creaking of his sleeping vital signs, but as I looked at him from my stiff vinyl chair a few feet away, he seemed alien and remote. I was as grief-stricken as the day I'd been told my parents were missing, and yet the person I missed was right in front of me.

"I'm so sorry," I whispered to his sleeping face. "I'm so sorry. How can you ever forgive me?"

I cried carefully, hoping no one would hear me. I thought about how cruelly I had argued with him in the last weeks, and I wanted to erase myself like a drawing. I wondered if it was moments like this that drove Joe Creekman to madness, that made him retreat from the world of people.

⚜

The evening wore on and still Uncle Alvin drowsed. I poked my head out of the room and asked a nurse if this was normal, and she said yes, he had been administered a few drugs that would make him sleepy and the only thing to do was let him snooze it off. She smiled down at me and told me I looked like I could use some dinner from the cafeteria.

My stomach turned at the very thought of food. I felt like I didn't deserve to eat. I had been too awful. And I was still afraid to leave Uncle Alvin's side, as well—though this time, it might have been the fear of myself getting lost in the labyrinthine hospital.

I tiptoed back into Uncle Alvin's room and closed the gargantuan door. The doors to the rooms were about as tall as the average, but double-wide to accommodate wheelchairs and beds, making them look like oversized gnome holes. The walls were lined with handrails, the buttons on the bedside TV remote/phone were oversized for the poorly sighted, and the handles and knobs in the private bathroom were extra large to accommodate arthritic or weak hands. Everything, including the modular vinyl visitors' furniture and the fat red table lamp on the battered nightstand, combined to make Uncle Alvin look smaller.

I studied the room's every minute detail, looking for something that would make it less frightening. Even the bright flowers on the wall clock were grim. All I could think was *Will I remember that flowered clock as the one in the hospital room where I lost Uncle Alvin?*

Why had it taken me seven years to realize I loved Uncle Alvin? We assume we love our relatives, naturally. But I'd never understood how much. How he might not have been the most demonstrative of parents, but he had been my surrogate parent nonetheless. He had never resented me for invading his life and his house. He had never made me feel unwelcome. He had incorporated me into his well-worn habits. He had done more than feed and clothe me; he had taught me, and teaching was the most precious gift I had associated with my mother. And I had rejected him in every possible way, short of openly telling him I hated him.

I ached with loneliness. I wanted support, a friend to appear from the other side of the curtain pulled around our portion of the room, and I wanted to feel his arm around my shoulder and my cheek against his shirt. I wanted someone to talk to about how I regretted neglecting Uncle Alvin so dreadfully. I wanted to tell Alvin, but he was asleep and I was afraid. I didn't want to be alone with myself and this awful corrosive feeling that was consuming me from the inside.

I stared at the curtain, trying to will this faceless, nameless friend into truth. Sometimes it was Max as I had known her before our fights, more often it was Bulfinch rounding that corner. I took Max out of my imagination and shook out her creases. I thought about the day under the tree with the notebook or the dim evening in my room trying to conjure knights, and I felt a deep stab of regret. Where was Max when I actually needed her?

I remembered that once she had given me her number on a little piece of note card. I had been wearing this very shirt—a shirt I rarely washed because I still tried to imagine it held the scent of home. I felt the breast pocket and there it was, Max's note card crinkled and soft at the edges. I crept to the other side of Uncle Alvin's bed and eased the phone on his hospital nightstand off its hook. Hunched over the receiver, as if to cradle its sound with my body, I dialed Max's number.

It rang three times. Then I heard, "Thank you for calling the George Peabody Library. No one is available to take your call at this time. If you'd like to leave a message ..."

I hung up. I convulsed a little tighter in my bent position, writhing with frustration. Why would Max give me a false number? I hated her, but I still needed her. I was more determined than ever to be the one to contact her first, in this one instance, when I finally needed her there in a real, in a solid way. I knew it was crazy, but I dialed one more number: Johns Hopkins University. I navigated my way through menus and extensions until I finally had the number I sought.

"Thomas Charlemagne," the weary voice of my professor answered. I had to steady myself for the conversation I knew would follow. I spoke up and identified myself.

"I'm really glad you're in the office," I continued, a desperate tinge to my relief.

"I stayed late to grade some papers. Speaking of which ..."

"I know. I'm sorry. I know I don't have any excuses left. I'm not calling to make any. I just need your help," I trailed off, my voice cracking unintentionally. He seemed to hear my distress, however, because after an irritated pause, he asked, "What's wrong?"

"My uncle's in the hospital. I need to call a friend, but I don't have her number. I was wondering if you could go on ISIS and look it up for me. She's in comparative literature." I gave him Max's full name.

"Hold on," he told me. "I'll look it up right now."

I heard him put the phone down. I was overwhelmed with gratitude. He was the only professor I knew who would do something like that, and promptly, too. Most professors were so adverse to using the school's contact and transcript database, ISIS, that they wouldn't log on to it if it was the only way to save their burning house. If it was their student's burning house, they wouldn't even turn the computer on.

A few minutes later, Professor Charlemagne picked up the phone again. There was a strange new note in his voice, slightly sad or slightly frightened.

"I'm sorry," he told me, "But I can't find her anywhere. You're sure she goes here?"

I only go to class when you don't. When you're not here, I don't exist.

"I'll try somewhere else," I said thickly. A numbness was spreading though my mouth.

"I'm truly sorry I couldn't help," Professor Charlemagne continued. "Is there anything else I can do?"

"No, thank you. Thanks again."

"I hope your uncle feels better soon. Let me know how things go."

"I will. Thanks again."

"Take care."

"Bye."

I listened to the distant dial tone before hanging up Uncle Alvin's bedside phone.

I knew where Max was.

She lived inside my mind.

My hands shook violently and I sat on them, biting my lips.

I was losing it, and I had just given myself away.

Our morning-distilled first conversation—who else had been there to see her? The afternoon under the pines and lilacs ... our rambles around campus ... had anyone else ever said hello to her? Where was she when we weren't in class together? *Nowhere.* I never talked to her aloud ... except when she upset me very much ... or try to introduce her to anyone ... except when I wasn't sure the other party was real either ... oh, God.

"Sometimes your wheels spin too fast for one girl," Uncle Alvin had said.

I tried saying it aloud for the first time, under my breath, in Uncle Alvin's hospital room: *This is Max, my imaginary friend. My only friend.* My only friend was imaginary.

I had just tried to call her. My mouth stretched and my breath wouldn't come, but I didn't cry or make a noise. I felt like I was imploding. This is what insanity feels like. I had finally crossed the last bridge. I was totally alone, and it had driven me crazy. Just when Uncle Alvin needed me to keep it together, I was losing my mind.

An imaginary friend couldn't comfort me when reality had chased everything else away. Max wouldn't call, Max wouldn't hold my hand through the night, Max wouldn't sit on the edge of Alvin's bed and smile over a bunch of fresh flowers, Max wouldn't be saving me tonight.

It must have been the stress that made me make that phone call, I told myself. Someone had knocked out the supporting studs in my brain, and it was now coming down on itself. *Extreme emotional distress,* I remembered a phrase from my one and only therapy session, back when my parents had been declared dead. *Extreme emotional distress can make us say and do crazy things. Center yourself. Lean on your friends. They know you and then can help you find normal again.*

That's what the therapist had said to me. That was before I'd made up Max. She didn't know that my "friend" was the crazy thing grief had done to me.

If I had been desperate enough to imagine Max and let the game get away with me that far, had anything—was it all—? I recoiled from the thought like it was a hot burner.

I was devastated, cold. There was no comfort. Curled tightly around my disappointment, I faded into sleep after a long blue while. I woke up after fitful napping in the stiff chair several hours later. I stood to stretch. My throat was rough and dry from the intense air conditioning, and I couldn't suppress a coughing fit.

Uncle Alvin's eyes slid open fuzzily, and he looked at me for a moment from his pillow. His exhaustion was terrifying, as if a ghost had replaced him inside his body.

"What time is it?" he croaked.

I looked around at the dismal flowered clock on the wall.

"1:30. Saturday morning."

Alvin looked briefly confused.

"They must have really put me under," he chuckled weakly.

"They want to hold onto you for a few more tests," I reminded him.

Alvin grunted and fell back onto his pillow.

"Hospitals always want to test you in the middle of the night," he grumbled. "There's no way to get any sleep."

I wanted to sit beside him and squeeze his hand, rearrange his bedclothes, and ask him how he was feeling or if he was scared. But I was frozen. Uncle Alvin and I were never physically demonstrative of affection. Instead, I awkwardly climbed back into my chair, perched on the edge of his vision as he lay. He followed me with his eyes.

"Go home, Rosie," he said abruptly. "Get some rest. I sleep just as well without supervision."

I wanted to explain to him that it would make me feel so much better just to sit there, thinking that at some point I could be useful, but he was right.

"What if they move you?" I asked, trying to sound calm, as if my fear were a joke.

"I'll call you in the morning," he said.

I stood, and lingered while he watched me. Then, pushing myself as if my feet were bricks, I shuffled to his bed and pressed my cheek to his forehead briefly.

"I'm sorry," I mumbled.

Then I left, staring steadily at the beige linoleum patchwork of the floor.

Would Bulfinch be there for me when I got home? I had the heartbreaking sense the answer was no. I couldn't shake the suspicion that this was the night everything was bound to fall away—that whether or not he had ever existed, he would have vanished by now, like my parents had, like Uncle Alvin threatened to do.

ℐℐ

When I got home I bolted for the attic. My mouth was dry and I felt dizzy.

The attic was a playground of shadows like it had been that night. And there was no Bulfinch. I moaned. I ran into the attic and searched every corner, as if he were playing hide-and-seek. I turned every light on. He was nowhere. I spun around, little pieces of me were scattering behind.

I was about to plunge down the stairs again when I saw him standing at the bottom, looking up inquisitively. I'm not sure if I ran down the stairs or rolled—I had a lot of bruises later that I couldn't account for—the next thing I remember is throwing my arms around his shoulders and burying my face in his shirt, standing a few steps up from him so I had to hunch down around him.

I was sobbing dry. I couldn't feel much of my face, but I could smell the strong salty scent of his skin and the mustiness of his clothes, and after a few moments I felt his arms awkwardly brace my back. With that small sign of comfort, the dam burst and real tears began to flow. I cried so hard my nose bled.

There was a sizeable patch of blood on his shirt by time he ushered me into the kitchen. I leaned over the sink while he ran a dishtowel under cold water. I leaned back and held it to my face, but I reached out one hand to grasp his arm. Even with him in my sight, I needed to continually touch him to reassure myself.

"Where's Joachim?" I croaked.

"In the garden. We heard the commotion this afternoon, but I advised self-concealment, since we were uncertain if it was part of your uncle's ordinary business, and our appearance might accomplish naught but lead to discovery. When you didn't appear at your usual time this evening, and silence pervaded the house, Joachim insisted on searching the place, reiterating his oath not to escape in the meantime. He must have had a change of heart in the last weeks, for he is very eager to defend his own prison. When we confirmed your absence, Joachim became convinced you were abducted by hostile neighbors and has been keeping watch ever since just outside the door. It took all of my reasoning and ... a few embellishments on my purported powers to convince him not to depart immediately in search of you."

Holding Bulfinch's hand, I walked to the back of the house and opened the door to Joachim.

I looked at the knight. In his eye I saw the same panic of desertion that had pounded through my veins moments earlier. He didn't look like a knight. He looked like a lost kid. And here he thought he had come riding to *my* rescue.

"This is the most good care I have found in here place," he said in halting Latin. Bulfinch had been teaching him. "I think if noisy girl-peasant go away now, I never find home and lost forever."

"I know the feeling," I said.

I was starting to feel raw, but with each breath came an adrenaline-shot sense of vitality, and after my tears the air was sweet like fresh water.

I explained to Joachim and Bulfinch that my uncle was unwell; that the sounds they had heard were the doctors coming to help him and that he was spending the night in the hospital. Joachim accepted the news gravely, with a pall of genuine concern. He promptly took his bow and marched back to return to his prison's open door. Bulfinch lingered. He had seen how shaken I was by the news, and he wouldn't leave my side.

I was unspeakably grateful. That night I couldn't sleep in my own room. It felt oddly cold in the June night, as if September had crept in early, and the darkness was maddening. I wanted to be close to the phone, so I slept on the couch in the living room with the reading lamp on. Bulfinch curled up next to me, his arm over my shoulder.

I looked up at him. I remembered the afternoon we'd met—or rather, I'd tackled him—when I had the idea of calling him Bulfinch as a way to dignify the name his bullies had given him. It had never occurred to me to ask another question instead.

"What do your friends call you?" I asked quietly.

"My only friend, Aefle, calls me Ed," he said. "But I don't mind Bulfinch all that much."

For the first time that night, I laughed, and drifted to sleep under a thin quilt that Bulfinch pulled over me, with Aunt Patti's knitting neatly in the basket by the chair across from us and the detritus of Uncle Alvin's collection snoring gently their literary dreams.

CHAPTER TWENTY-TWO

#562: Pars Phlebotinum

BULFINCH SNORTED AT the sound of the phone and began to sit up, dragging my head up with him, and as my eyes creaked open on the new morning, yesterday fell back into place. I groped for the phone and answered croaking.

It was Uncle Alvin—they were discharging him within the hour. His tests were good. I felt my entire body sigh with relief, but at the same time I felt like the most miserably useless person on earth. I asked if he wanted me to come get him, and he said no, he'd just get a cab home, but perhaps I could fix him a cup of tea. Decaffeinated. When he hung up, I launched into the kitchen as if I'd been sent by the king to excavate the ancient chamomile I knew hid somewhere in the upper cabinets.

Bulfinch followed me into the kitchen. I explained the call to him, and he asked if he should disappear upstairs before Alvin returned.

"No," I said, with conviction. "No, you stay down here."

Bulfinch's eyebrows shot up, but he didn't question me. We lowered ourselves tensely into chairs and waited, listening to the water boil, until we saw through the window Uncle Alvin's cab pull up. My heart hammered with a thousand worries. I shot up again and ran outside to help him.

In the brilliant sunshine, Uncle Alvin still retained some of the shrunken look he'd had last night; it lingered in the pockets under his eyes. But in his usual clothes, he already seemed a little more like himself.

"Good morning, Rosie," he said quietly as I looped my arm under his shoulder. I felt him heavily lean into me. In his other hand was an aluminum cane with a clawed bottom. We took the front step slowly.

When we entered the house, Bulfinch emerged from the kitchen. He followed us to the living room with a steaming mug for Alvin. Uncle Alvin didn't bat an eye.

When he was settled into his armchair, I took a deep breath and said, "Uncle Alvin, there's someone you should meet. This is Adelbert Lufthild Baldfunke, but we just call him Bulfinch. He's from the Middle Ages."

"Oh, there's another one," Uncle Alvin replied in Latin. "I'd thought there might be two, but I only met your other friend."

You could have knocked me over with a feather. Bulfinch was equally stunned. We must have looked pretty comical because Uncle Alvin had a good chuckle at our expense.

"Really, Rosie," he wheezed. "The first time I saw Joachim, he was dropping from the fire escape into the garden in broad daylight." It must have been that first morning, I thought, the day he had escaped while I was at the library. "He was carrying one of your books," Alvin continued, "And he looked very peculiar in his armor. I thought you had made an interesting friend and chose to hide him from me."

I groaned. So he had known all along.

"The second time I met Joachim," Alvin went on, "You had disappeared, I can only assume to the library to cram that paper your professor called about the next day. In the evening after you left, Joachim ambled down, casual as sunshine, into the kitchen to fetch himself some food. It seems you'd been neglecting him sorely. Now, seeing a strange man in plate armor browsing my kitchen piqued my curiosity, so I asked him a few questions.

"Like you must have, I tried several languages, but unlike you, I had a bit of German left from my school days and I could grasp a general sense of what he told me. It was quite a tale, but his dress, his confusion at the objects of modern life, and your secretiveness convinced me it was true. When I heard about the supernatural monk, I could only assume you had another companion who had accompanied you out of the house. I made what seems to have been the correct assumption that your play on his superstition was a ruse to keep him from embarking on any other adventures, so I played along. I told him that what he said was true and also that we were an outpost in a very evil city, and that as a knight he could begin to atone for his sins by volunteering his guard to our home. I convinced him the best vantage was back in the attic, and I felt secure that he'd be occupied for many days keeping watch up there."

I was even more stunned. I didn't know Uncle Alvin had that kind of inventiveness in him. Bulfinch grinned eagerly, happy to have found a kindred spirit. So I wheeled on my medieval friend.

"Why didn't Joachim ever say anything about this to you?" I interrogated.

Bulfinch blushed and stared at his toes.

"He mentioned something," he mumbled. "I just assumed he was making it up."

I groaned. Bulfinch was such an embellisher, of course he would assume Joachim was one too.

"That was when I proposed the chess games," Bulfinch continued. "I thought perhaps mentioning contact with your Uncle was an overture to an escape, maybe even aided by that gentleman, so I concocted something to hold him honor-bound a bit longer."

"By that second visit, I began to become concerned," Uncle Alvin retrieved the thread of his story. "Clearly you had been hiding these boys for several days, and you didn't show any signs of telling me."

"Why didn't you just bring it up yourself?" I blurted, before realizing he had. "I mean, why didn't you just tell me what you knew?"

"I wanted *you* to tell me," Alvin responded as his eyes drooped. "I wanted you to introduce me when you saw fit. I told Joachim to make my home his own, but you've been here seven years and you've never done the same."

I didn't have a reply. Uncle Alvin sighed sleepily and let his eyes drift shut.

"Maybe this afternoon you can start bringing my things back downstairs," he murmured. "Then we can discuss what to do with our guests."

In a few minutes, he was peacefully sleeping. Bulfinch and I crept upstairs not to hide, but to let Alvin doze in peace.

❧❧

That night, Bulfinch, Joachim, and I gathered around Uncle Alvin in the living room. In the middle of our group, I placed the box containing *Pars Phlebotinum.*

I took a deep breath and squeezed Bulfinch's hand. He looked the way I felt. Joachim, too, looked frightened, but less sad.

Uncle Alvin picked up the book. He ran his hand over the cover. At first my breath caught to see him touching it so casually, but clearly it was harmless.

"Joe loves this book," Uncle Alvin said. "One of a kind. He thought it was amusing, with all its typographical errors. All the page numbers are reversed." He chuckled while he flipped through it. "I can see what you and your mother found fascinating about that page. I can only imagine her glee if she'd had a chance to see the book itself."

He handed it to me. I stared at the cover, still too scared to open it for myself.

"Go ahead, Rosie," Alvin encouraged me gently. "It's for the best."

I opened the cover slowly.

Before I could turn the pages, a picture fluttered out. Crumpled, torn, strangely flimsy, it was a snapshot featured in a faded tourist pamphlet for historic landmarks in a small German town. The couple in the picture were my parents, exactly as I had last seen them.

Written in a shaky hand at the top was a note from Joe Creekman: "Two people of our acquaintance, I believe."

I was dumbfounded. But Bulfinch's reaction was wholly unexpected. He wailed and threw himself off of the couch and onto his knees, begging forgiveness in a choked voice. I was so startled that I couldn't think to ask him what he had done wrong, and he was so contrite he couldn't gather the words to explain why.

Joachim and my uncle watched in bewilderment—the knight, suddenly concerned that his ticket home was expiring, while Alvin's confusion was more aloof, as if he had seen enough surprises in the story that he accepted it as his share.

Bulfinch and I, however, were still very capable of vocal amazement. Our first questions to each other tumbled out at the same time:

"Bulfinch, do you know my parents?"

"Are those people your mother and father?"

Now I was the one choking for air. Bulfinch recognized my parents. Bulfinch had seen my parents.

They were alive somewhere in time. They were alive and maybe they had never meant to leave me at all.

Maybe they missed me. Maybe they missed me as much as I missed them. Oh, God, I missed them.

I didn't feel the tears running down my cheeks, at first, when I asked him, "Bulfinch, how do you know my parents?"

"It is my sin, it is my sin," he muttered, inconsolably. "I have wronged them. You will never forgive me."

Even through my own tumultuous emotions, I began to feel a little impatient with his inarticulateness. It was the one time Bulfinch didn't seem willing to tell a tale.

"You have to tell me," I begged him. "I'll forgive you, I promise I will, but you have to tell me. I can't forgive you until I know."

Bulfinch looked up with me with such an open, pleading look that I knew what I said was true at that moment, that I would forgive him almost anything. But I still took a deep breath, dreading whatever was to come.

"Yes, I knew your parents," he said. "They came to the abbey last winter, a few months before Joachim arrived. They sought me specifically. They said they had heard of my reputation as an artist with words, and they wanted me to write a very specific story. They wanted me to write a story about themselves. Nothing long or elaborate; a simple story about two gentlepeople who loved and lived ... who had a child ... and loved her ..." he stopped suddenly. "You," he finished.

My heart leapt. Had they tried to use Bulfinch to draw me into the past to join them there, however they had got there?

Why didn't it work?

And like a cold flash of ice gripping my heart, I realized what Bulfinch needed forgiveness for.

"But I was vain," he wailed, creeping toward me even as he saw my eyes hardening. "I was so flattered by their praise of my writing that I took it upon myself to make their story more interesting. 'Write it, Adelbert, and it will be real,' they told me, with such confidence that I nearly believed they spoke literally and not figuratively. And so convinced was I of my prowess that instead of enshrining their memory in a simple, affectionate tale as they had requested, I thought I paid them a compliment by spinning it into a romance, by turning them, in fiction, into clever bandits whose story would entertain travelers on a cold night."

My veins froze.

"I felt remorse," he whined, "for disobeying their wishes, a remorse that only grew as the strangeness of the past few days unfolded. But now I am convinced it was my punishment to be sent here in this manner, to be so removed from all I know, to be cast into a world where I know as little, as is only fitting for one who felt he knew so much in the world he left behind. There is one last transgression I committed against the promise I made to your parents."

I wanted to slap him for telling me all of this in his grandiloquent style. I wanted to tell him how hurtful and insulting it was for him to use my parents' story as a prop for his ego. But I tried to contain it all. I had to know every crumb of any message my parents might have tried to send me, and I couldn't afford to intimidate him if it would discourage him from telling all.

"They told me that one day I would write a story about a man sent far away, out of his time and place by supernatural means. They asked that, instead of writing about that man, I should write about them. But by the time the fancy struck me to write that particular story, they had faded from my mind as a kind but unremarkable couple, and the knight who had irritated my pride also inspired my imagination."

Bulfinch looked up at me expectantly. Silence blanketed the room after his story wound to an end. It was my own gurgling sniffle that broke it and reminded me of where I was. The dam burst, and I was on my feet.

"You could have given my parents back," I shouted at him. "They wanted to come back to me. *They wanted to come back to me.* They asked you to send them back to me. And you screwed it up. You—you—you destroyed everything I love."

I don't know whether I shouted or whispered those last words. I only know I left them as a trail behind me, as I ran up the stairs away from the three people staring at me below, in a tight circle around a book we had all forgotten.

I sat in my room. It might have been an hour or five minutes. Time didn't mean a lot to me anymore.

I was staring at my mother's last postcard to me. I read and reread her gentle slanting handwriting.

Darling,

One day you'll come here and see this picture in real life. I hope I'm there, too. Today your father and I are taking a little boat to a beach a local told us about. I have a blanket and the manuscript Dad bought me from that dealer on the Continent, near the ruined abbey in the picture on this card. We're going to read it in the sun, like you and I read on nice days in the backyard. I thought it would be the perfect way to open it for the first time. I can pretend that I'm with my little girl, too. We love and miss you very much.

Love,
Mom (and Dad)

They were that close to being with me again. They were that close, and Bulfinch had screwed it up. I held the postcard to my chest awkwardly and rocked back and forth with it. I used to hold books that way, against my chest, when I ran with them into the backyard, when I lived with my parents.

The pieces put themselves together in my mind. My parents had found Bulfinch's personal notebook. His writing had the power to transport people; and if they had started reading at the beginning, it would have taken them years to catch up with him as he was poised to write the tale of Joachim. Seven years that I had spent waiting in Alvin's house, waiting beyond hope or reason for the message that finally came.

I sobbed so hard I didn't feel Uncle Alvin's arms around me until I blew my nose on his shirt. At first I thought it was the sheet and I had fallen on the bed because I had never been held by him before.

For the first time, instead of disappearing when I began to cry, Uncle Alvin had appeared.

"Stupid girl," he murmured affectionately. "You get what you want, and I have to come up and explain it to you."

"How can you possibly say this is what I wanted?" I growled. It seemed obvious to me that this moment was the antithesis of everything I had longed for for seven years.

"Think, Rosie," Alvin continued. "What have I been teaching you to do all this time? Think. Adelbert was going to write that story about Joachim no matter what. The fact that you saw it on that page from that book tells you so—it was passed down for hundreds of years, and your parents knew too. They never asked Adelbert to send them back in that story. He told you so to make you feel better."

"How is that supposed to make me feel better?" I whined. "Why do you want me to believe they didn't want to come back to me?" I threw myself facedown on my bed like a petulant teenager.

Uncle Alvin sighed. I didn't know then how much love and patience was summed up in that sigh, but he continued matter-of-factly.

"Rosie, your parents were imperfect people. They sometimes did foolish things, and sometimes very foolish things. Stealing from your father's company was one. But what they did out of love, they did out of deep, genuine love, even if those things were foolish too. Perhaps they thought that if they remained in the past, their crimes would never be scrutinized and you would be spared the pain of seeing your parents go to jail. Maybe they just assumed it was impossible for them to return."

I peeled my face up from the pillow and looked at Alvin.

"Before you can forgive your parents, you must admit their crime," he said. "They loved you, and they wanted to send you a message of their love. Bulfinch cares for you, and tonight, when he told you their story, he wanted to give them back to you, too."

I looked up at Alvin in silence: steady and sheltering, real and protective and practical as the house that I loved too, the house where I had grown up, this house in Hampden with the stuffy attic and creaky fire escape, my home.

"You shouldn't have walked up all those stairs," I whispered to him. He only smiled. I tried to think of the last time I had seen him smile, and I couldn't remember.

"What now?" I croaked.

"This story has an ending," he replied. "And there are two people waiting downstairs for us to read it."

℞

We sat in a tighter circle around the coffee table, my hand in Bulfinch's as I paged through the book to 120. Before I could glance at it, I squeezed my eyes shut tight and focused on the feeling of Bulfinch's hand around mine. I took a deep breath, opened my eyes, and looked down.

At the top of page 120, where the end of the monk's story about a disappearing knight should have been, there was only the word:

LACUNA

I turned to Bulfinch. I knew he understood it; the word was directly from the Latin: a gap, a missing passage. The ending of his story was lost.

"You never finished it," I whispered.

I turned the book to Uncle Alvin so he could see. He grunted once and then said, "Do you still have the blank page from the letter?"

I thought carefully. If Max was imaginary so had been her taunt—I had never looked for it in my notebook after she had waved her "copy" in front of me.

Upstairs, the original letter was easy enough to locate, magically cleared. It fit perfectly into the book.

"Get Bulfinch a pen," Alvin said. I got up again and headed for the kitchen, where I knew Uncle Alvin's treasured fountain pen lived in the desk. Bulfinch followed me.

I dug the Waterman in its velvet case out of the desk drawer, and handing it to Bulfinch, our fingers touched again.

In the space between us, a thousand dust motes danced with the microscopic wind of our movement.

"I'm sorry," I whispered. But I also knew there had never been much reason for him to stay with me. There must have been something else more important. There usually was.

Bulfinch only smiled gently and led me back to the gathering in the other room.

We sat in silence for ten minutes while he covered the front and back of the page with large, blocky script. In silence, he passed the book back to me.

Before I had a chance to start reading, Joachim dropped from his seat on one knee swiftly and, picking up my hand, kissed it with elaborate gallantry. Then, turning to Uncle Alvin, he grasped his forearm and shook it in a medieval knight's salute.

When he looked back and me and nodded that he was ready, I began to read.

The knight at first was overcome by a very madness of rage and confusion, but this subsiding he became determined to prevail and prove himself worthy of return to his beloved home. In this strange and new land, he encountered many adversaries that threatened his life and the accomplishment of his self-reform: steel monsters, gawking peasants, and antagonistic constabulary. Yet there was one home open to him despite all adversity: the home of a young maiden determined to help the lost and weary traveler reverse the spell that had seized him from his own land.

Meanwhile, I, his humble chronicler, watched these events with mine own eyes and can attest to their veracity as greater than any other story I have yet recorded. For during a long fortnight, this maiden cared for the knight while she sought the magic text to conclude his tale. Finally, after much pain and travail, she opened the enchanted tome and read aloud these words, which returned Sir Joachim to his rightful home:

For on the fourteenth night of his enchantment, the gilded saint returned to Sir Joachim's vision and filled him with awe and joy, for no longer would fear or incivility raise his temper to strangers. And the saint said he had fulfilled his penance, and had grown from a resentful boy into a honorable knight most worthy of the name of chivalry, and his past transgressions of manners and charm would be forgiven as long as he lived in civility and kindness all his life. Then, with a blinding flash of sapphire light, the saint transported Sir Joachim to his home, where he prospered many years as a generous lord and noble defender of his King, with a bounteous family and a hearty eldest son.

I, Adelbert Lufthild Baldfunke, known among friends as Ed and among my closest companions as Bulfinch, do certify this story as true, for I have witnessed it with my own eyes, and record it as I saw it

*while I remain, in the home of the maiden, in the Year
of our Lord of the unimaginable future.*

When I looked up, the knight was gone.

Uncle Alvin had a faraway look in his eyes. I felt a sense of the end, relief and sadness mixed, settle over my heart like a cloak. But then Uncle Alvin quirked his mouth into a half-smile and darted his eyes to the left of me.

There, still beside me, sat Bulfinch, biting his lip and twirling the pen between his fingers.

"It worked," he squeaked. "Thank goodness. I was never a very good monk, anyway."

Laughing and crying, I said, "I thought you said this place was your punishment!" Laughing harder, I said, "I thought you wanted to go home!"

"No, no, my stupidity was my punishment," he smiled in response. "This place is a blessing. It has indoor plumbing."

I hugged him so hard I thought I'd dislocate my arms.

CHAPTER TWENTY-THREE

THE END OF THE CATALOGUE

MY CHILDHOOD HOME in White Hall was torn down that summer. The family that bought it wanted to start over. When I try to remember it now, I can't see it clearly. It isn't because I was too young, at the age of twelve, to form an impression of it; it's because the impression was so deep it cut past physical detail and left an imprint of pure emotion. I remember how the grass of the backyard made me smile as it tickled my toes. I remember the late afternoon light making the dining room with its lavishly outdated wallpaper look like a sultan's palace. I remember Mom in the kitchen on summer nights and the small trail of mugs and books and fluttering papers that followed her there and every place she went. I see my parents as blurry forms of love and longing.

It's August now, as I write our story. I've struggled like a monk with the brush and pen in dim light to illuminate it. Professor Charlemagne couldn't save me from academic probation, but I'm making up for my failed semester with summer coursework, and I've recorded the story of our adventure in stolen snatches between the first serious study to which I've ever applied myself.

After Joachim disappeared, Bulfinch told me why he had really cursed him.

"The night he visited the monastery, in the refectory during supper he stepped on my robe and made me fall into the stew," he told me. "I was very unhappy about that."

But one man's curse was another man's blessing; in addition to bringing him into a home of like minds, Bulfinch told me later that night that the future gave him a second chance to pursue his passion.

"I may have slightly exaggerated a few aspects concerning my prospects at the University of Paris," he began in his usual innocent tone. "As I recall, I may have neglected to tell you a few details of that story. You see, I had submitted my exercises in logic to several of the more prominent professors there. I received a letter informing me that they contained too much of what they referred to as 'undisciplined embellishment and fictive fancy.' And so my career as a philosopher was ... postponed until I could provide more sophisticated work."

He eased his defenses a little and smiled at me.

"Apparently my hypothetical exercises illustrating some questions of ethics and governance tended to stray from the question and into the realm of romance. I had been especially proud of one in which I demonstrated the moral conflict between justice and mercy by depicting justice as a many-ridged dragon and mercy as a fair maid in white robes whose word, and her word only, could placate the beast. The dean of Aristotelian ethics wrote to me that he had used my page to blow his nose."

Oddly, Bulfinch's real story was comforting to me as I embarked on my own studies. I brought him with me to the library often, so he could begin to fill his mind with the knowledge he had craved for so long—knowledge that fed not just his mind but his voracious imagination. I was learning to acquire more than just good study habits. Once, when I found myself behind Allison in line at the library cafe, I actually brought myself to smile at her. I still couldn't bring myself to enjoy her chatter. But I was beginning to realize what had always made me socially uncomfortable was not other people, but myself.

We never spent whole days away from the house, however. Now, if Uncle Alvin was home, one of us stayed with him too, to make sure he was comfortable and to be with him in case of a second "heart event," though I gave him my time more freely now because I think he had also longed for the companionship that he had refused to ask for.

Our adventure also inspired him to get back in touch with Vita and to begin writing again to Joe Creekman. Vita is making plans to visit Baltimore in the fall. She told me on the phone last week that she finally felt secure leaving Joe's business in her secretary's hands for a week while she took a much-needed vacation. Joe had sent her his book with a note inside just for her that she had removed before forwarding the *Pars Phlebotinum* to us: he simply wrote "Thank you. I feel like I am home now."

Now that my story is over, I'm sending it to my old address. This time I know the direction is correct, it just doesn't exist any more. I don't know you, but I know that eventually curiosity will overwhelm you when you can't find your letter's true owner, and you'll open it and take this manuscript out. You'll hold it in your hand and feel its weight and wonder who sent it. Then you'll begin to read.

And maybe, if the saint of our story is still watching, it will make my mother and my father, imperfect and beautiful as I knew and loved them as a child in our vanished home, as real to you as my letter made Bulfinch's knight real to me.

ACKNOWLEDGMENTS

More thanks than I can fit onto a page go to:

Victoria Marini, my agent, who gave me a chance, helped shape this book, and has believed in me for years despite rejections and setbacks galore.

Libby Sternberg, my mom, my first and best writing teacher, promotion guru, and martini provider.

Lindsey Reinstrom, who edited this book with unflagging cheer; Elizabeth Goss, a childhood friend who grew up to become a gifted designer and created the cover for this book; and Jerri Corgiat, a family friend and book description whiz.

The friends and family whose encouragement helped me get this story onto a page, and those pages into a reader's hands.

ABOUT THE AUTHOR

Hannah Sternberg lives in Washington, DC, with an ill-fated succession of bamboo plants all named Beatrice. In 2009, she graduated from The Johns Hopkins University with a major in Film and Media Studies and a minor in Writing Seminars, feeling like the most unemployable girl in the world. Somehow, despite this ignominious start, she has worked for several years in the book business, as an editor and marketing professional for several major publishers. She is the co-founder and senior editor of Istoria Books, a boutique publisher of literary and genre fiction. In addition to writing, she spends her time reciting Proust front to back from memory, and trying to mix the perfect cocktail. One of those two hobbies is made up.

Queens of All the Earth, Hannah Sternberg's first novel, was released by Bancroft Press in October 2011. Early reviews called it "exquisite" and "completely addicting."

Learn more about Hannah at her website, where you can find giveaways, snippets of coming work, writing advice, and more!

www.HannahSternberg.com

Bonus material ahead! Up next: *Bulfinch*-themed reading suggestions, and a free excerpt from Hannah's first novel, *Queens of All the Earth*.

FURTHER READING

I couldn't pretend to be a historian, even on Halloween.

I started writing *Bulfinch* while I was taking a year-long medieval history lecture to fulfill a degree requirement. I was surprised by how quickly I fell in love with the field once I actually started attending class, which was unfortunately about halfway through the second semester.

I hope *Bulfinch* inspires you to explore the Middle Ages. To start, try some fun and quirky books that Uncle Alvin would read to the geraniums all day long.

The Letters of Abelard and Heloise tell the fantastically gripping true story of two forbidden lovers who were forced to become a monk and a nun when their secret marriage was thwarted. My favorite edition is the Penguin Classics translation by Betty Radice. (Original written sometime in the middle of the twelfth century.)

Anna Comnena's **Alexiad** contains an eyewitness account of the knights of the First Crusade, written by the daughter of the Emperor of Byzantium. It's just one small slice of her adventure-filled biography of her father. Comnena is a cool, witty, fearless observer of one of history's most tumultuous episodes. (Written in 1148.)

If Geoffrey Chaucer's **Canterbury Tales** traumatized you in high school, give them another shot with a bit more patience as an adult. They're sometimes laugh-out-loud funny, and nearly always illuminating. Chaucer was pretty much writing the *Parks and Recreation* of his day -- funny, short stories about average people, that picked out the highlights, and lowlights, of human behavior. (Written in the late 14th century.)

But if you really want to let your imagination run wild, run no further than **Bulfinch's Mythology**. Thomas Bulfinch was a banker with a hidden passion for classical and medieval mythology. He lovingly cataloged the most famous myths and legends of the Greek, Roman, and medieval periods into three volumes that popularized the study of ancient myth in nineteenth-century America. Edith Hamilton came along in the 1940s and overcame him in popularity with her more pared-down retellings, and it was probably her slim *Mythology* that you read in grade school. But Bulfinch paved the way, with the express purpose of making it possible for average readers to learn, and love, the great stories of the past. ***The Age of Chivalry, or Legends of King Arthur*** by Thomas Bulfinch was published in 1858. His ***Legends of Charlemagne, or Romance of the Middle Ages*** was published in 1863.

FREE FIRST CHAPTER OF *QUEENS OF ALL THE EARTH*

CHAPTER 0: IT MAY NOT ALWAYS BE SO

AT CORNELL UNIVERSITY in upstate New York, a thousand freshmen milled through a dozen entry booths, collecting keys and pamphlets and signing waivers, meeting their roommates, bickering with their parents, then hugging their parents when they hoped their roommates weren't looking.

In Williamsburg, Virginia, a rented van waited, packed tight with the fruits of a shopping spree. Virtually everything inside was new, much of it still in its original packaging. Unflinching summer sunlight made the van's contents appear chintzy, forlorn.

A hastily parked car straddled the grass beside the driveway of the house where the van waited. The front door of the house stood slightly open.

"We know it's not physical," the doctor upstairs told Miranda Somerset. "Like the paramedics told you, her vitals are normal. The problem is in the mind."

The man, Dr. Simons, was a family friend from the College of William and Mary, where Miranda's mother worked. He was primarily an academic psychologist. At first, Miranda had called nine-one-one, but then she had panicked when the paramedics had told her they couldn't compel a legal adult to undergo psychiatric evaluation if she wasn't a threat to herself or others. The paramedics had left quietly, with a deflated sense of emergency, but Miranda's anxiety had only risen. She had called her mother, who was giving a paper in Middlebury, for some shred of advice, and her mother had told her to call Dr. Simons.

"Is there something you can give her? Valium or something? Something to get her through it?" Miranda asked him. "Just to get her out of bed? I'm sure as soon as she starts moving, she'll feel better."

"Miranda," said the man with the patience of one used to negotiating with denial, "she's had a full psychotic break. She isn't going anywhere."

"Move-in ends at 5 p.m.," Miranda said, unaware of the tear rolling down her cheek.

In the bedroom beyond the door where Miranda and Dr. Simons stood, the August sun sluiced through the gap where the blinds didn't drop down all the way, making a hard bright line on the floor. The mug of coffee Miranda had brought upstairs for her sister sat cold as granite on the nightstand. Olivia lay like a rock on her bed. Her eyes, peeled, stared at the ceiling. Beads of perspiration stood round and perfect on her forehead, though the room was cool. She didn't move.

Her left hand clutched a book from her childhood, *A Swiftly Tilting Planet*, a time-travel adventure. Her index finger held her place between the pages. Miranda had not been able to remove the book from her hands, and Dr. Simons, when he had arrived, had advised against trying.

"She shouldn't be alone," Dr. Simons said, glancing at Olivia.

"I can take another day off work," Miranda said. Miranda, seven years older than her sister, lived in Arlington, Virginia, where she worked as an accountant for an insurance company.

"Good. Talk to her. Play music she likes. Bring her food. Let her smell it," Dr. Simons said. "She's in there somewhere. My guess is she'll come out again sooner rather than later. Call me again tomorrow."

"Are you sure there isn't anything you can give her?"

"There's nothing physically wrong with her," the doctor repeated. "And I can't prescribe anything until she's undergone a full psychological evaluation. I wouldn't want to, even if I could. We don't know what we're dealing with until she decides to open up and start talking about it. Could be major depression, could be bipolar disorder." He took off his glasses and cleaned them on a corner of his jacket. "But considering her history, and your family's history, it's most probably nothing more than brief reactive psychosis. In that case, I'd recommend avoiding medication and letting her rest and recover at her own pace, with the help of therapy."

In the bedroom, Olivia heard but didn't hear the words being said about her. She had heard the metronomic alarm, steady and faithful like her breathing, but she also hadn't heard it, as if she were buried somewhere deep below the ocean, where all this sound and outside sensation fused into a solid block, a barrier between herself and now.

She had already been awake for an hour when the alarm had gone off, watching the ceiling grow from a pale shadow to a crisp white constellation of bubbles. Her alarm had wailed for another hour before Miranda had stormed into her room to wake her up.

The shouting. The pleading. The phone calls. The pounding on the stairs. Olivia had heard and not heard them. Her eyes were not glassy, but intense and focused.

"Can't you stay a little longer?" Miranda asked Dr. Simons. "I don't want to be . . ." She didn't finish the sentence. "I'm worried if she gets any worse," she said.

Dr. Simons looked at his watch.

"I can stay another hour or so," he said.

The freshmen of Cornell University were plugging in their microwaves, discovering which of their desk toys had broken, and comparing video game consoles. Their residence advisors were completing complicated checklists on battered clipboards. In another hour, many of the freshmen would disperse to find lunch, hoping they'd be able to find their way back to their rooms again.

Olivia didn't leave her room. She didn't move or speak all that morning. She did not set aside her book or remove her finger from the page it marked.

Dr. Simons sent one of his graduate students to sit by Olivia's bed in the afternoon, while Miranda unloaded the rental van and returned it. Dr. Simons picked Miranda up from the rental facility and took her home. She arrived to the sound of children's playful screams from the inflatable pool next-door.

That evening, as if she'd sensed the specter of the van was gone, Olivia sighed and turned her face to the side.

Dr. Simons and his graduate student went home.

That night, their mother called and asked Miranda to hold the phone to Olivia's ear.

"This is perfectly natural," their mother said. "Most adolescents fear the onset of adulthood. You'll come out of it, honey. In the meantime, let Miranda feed you some supper, okay?"

Olivia's silence was her only response.

That night, the freshmen of Cornell acted like they were too cool to wish they were at home.

The Somersets' neighbors' children slept, perfectly convinced no day could be as wonderful as today, except tomorrow.

Olivia slept that night, white under the sheets.

To continue reading, pick up a copy of *Queens of All the Earth* from your favorite book retailer, or download it from the Kindle store.

3/19/15

Made in the USA
San Bernardino, CA
17 September 2014